RIDE OR DYE

AIMEE NICOLE WALKER

DEDICATION

To the Dye Hards,

Thank you for taking this journey with Josh, Gabe, and me. You are my ride or die, and I am forever grateful.

XOXO

ONE

Josh

"This kind of feels like old times," Chaz softly said during lunch in the kitchenette at the salon.

"Except you'll be returning to your house to work on your next best seller instead of the receptionist desk out front," Mere told him before spooning more chicken noodle soup in her mouth.

"And Mere is going home to prop up her feet and rest up for the biggest adventure of her life," I said, pointing to her rounded baby belly. "Speaking of which, I'm going to need you to have her before I go on Gabe's surprise vacation. We purposely timed the trip for two weeks after your due date. You're not cooperating, Mere. Uncle Josh cannot miss the birth of his niece."

"Ew, not the third person again," Meredith said. It was a long-running joke between us about a boy she dated in school who had referred to himself in the third person. It always creeped her out. "You're crazy if you think I want this *kid* out of me less than you do. I'm ready to go right now, but someone has other ideas. A week past my due date and not even two centimeters dilated." Mere and Harley decided not to learn the sex of their baby during their ultrasounds, but I knew she was having a girl. I was never wrong either. While others played it safe with neutral colors for her baby shower presents, I boldly gifted her frilly pink dresses with matching shorts to wear beneath.

"How much longer will they let this drag out?" Chaz asked. "You look…" His words broke off while he searched for the right thing to say.

"The novelist who can't find the words, Mere," I teased.

"I must look frightening then," Mere said, smiling broadly at Chaz who squirmed in his seat.

"I'm just learning to think before I blurt things out," Chaz said.

"Where's the fun in that?" I teased. "Nothing made my day more than when you stepped on your dick."

"I don't think that's how the phrase goes?" Mere said after a good giggle.

"It works here," I countered. "Besides, you might not be married and raising a son with Doctor Dimples if it weren't for your uncanny ability to say the worst possible things at the worst possible times."

"True," Mere and Chaz both said.

"You look radiant even if you feel like you've been pregnant for nine years instead of nine months, Mere," Chaz said. "The old me would've found a way to screw it up and imply otherwise."

"I would've known what you meant, sweetie."

"This does feel like old times," I told them. "I wouldn't say those times were better though. I wouldn't trade the chaotic home I'll enter tonight for anything."

"Same," Mere said, rubbing her belly.

"It is nice just to have time for the three of us, isn't it?" Chaz asked. "We need to do this more often. We still see each other every Sunday, but it's not the same."

"Come over for dinner tonight," I said. "We'll splash around in the pool and grill out yummy food."

"The pool does sound nice," Meredith said wistfully. "The humidity makes this July weather feel like a hundred degrees." I had invited her to use the pool as much as she wanted, but she didn't want to impose.

Chaz glanced at his watch then got to his feet. "I need to head out and pick up Mark and Daniel from basketball camp. This is Kyle's early night at the animal hospital, so we can make it. What time do you want us there?"

"Does five or five thirty work for you?" I asked. It would give us time to swim for a while before dinner.

"Sounds perfect," Mere said, pushing herself to her feet. "I'm going to head home and take a nap so I'm refreshed for later. It won't be long before the swimming pool is off-limits for—" Mere stopped suddenly and looked at me with wide eyes. "Oh." She cupped her hand beneath her round belly and looked down like she couldn't believe what was happening. "Ohhhhhh."

"Oh shit," Chaz said, looking down at the floor. "Her water just broke. It's time!"

"Oh!" Meredith gasped like she couldn't comprehend it was real. Her soft response turned into a long, keening moan. "Ohhhhhhhhhhh."

"What's happening?" Chaz asked. "Should she be in pain already?"

I rounded the table and reached for Meredith's hands. The only thing I knew about labor and childbirth was from when our twins were born. Their mother was induced and her labor closely monitored, so I had no idea how to answer his question.

"Ohhhhhh," Meredith moaned again. "It hurts so bad. There's so much pressure." Meredith bursting into tears spurred me into action.

"Mere, have a seat to relieve the pressure. I'm going to call Harley and have him meet us at the hospital. Okay?"

Meredith cried out in pain and clutched her abdomen. "No time, Josh."

"What?" Chaz and I asked at the same time.

"She's coming now!" Meredith exclaimed.

"Ha! You agree that you're having a girl."

"You convinced me, Jazz." Meredith released a series of short breaths. "I love this salon, but I never pictured having my baby here."

"Here? Right now?" I asked, sounding much calmer than I felt. The line from *Gone with the Wind* echoed in my mind, but I put a modern spin on it. I didn't know jack about birthing babies.

"I think so. God! This hurts so fucking much."

"What's going on?" asked a voice I never thought I'd be happy to hear.

"Trent!" I said in relief. Thank God he had a hair appointment. He did a rotation in obstetrics and was present when Sally Ann gave birth to Adrianna. "Meredith's water broke, and she's in a lot of pain. She says there's a lot of pressure too."

"Pressure? Do you feel like your body is trying to push the baby out?" he asked, squatting down beside her.

"Mmm hmm," Meredith said, biting her lip. I moved around to the other side of her to hold her hand, hoping it would give her some comfort.

Trent looked over his shoulder and addressed Chaz. "Will you

4

please ask Dare to dial 9-1-1 and have them send an ambulance. It's better to err on the side of caution than assume she can ride in a car without mishap."

"And call Harley," I told Chaz.

Trent looked back at Meredith and offered her a composed smile. "You're going to be just fine, honey. I know this is awkward, but will you let me examine you to assess how close you are to delivering this baby?"

"Like I care who sees my vag at this point," Mere said, turning in her chair. I repositioned mine too so she could recline against my chest. That way I could offer her comfort without seeing the aforementioned vag. I'd look if she needed me to, but we had a trained professional on hand.

"I can't wait to meet your daughter," I whispered in Meredith's ear as she tried to breathe through the pain. I hoped to distract her just in case she found the idea of Trent removing her underwear and looking up her dress more awkward than she let on.

"You're so sure, aren't you?" Mere asked.

"I've never been wrong before," I reminded her.

"Whoa, that's a lot of hair," Trent said suddenly.

"What the fuck?" Meredith asked.

"Damn, Trent," I snarled. "You try lawn maintenance with a baby belly in the way."

"Not on her...um, vagina," he stumbled. "I was talking about the baby's head. She's crowning."

"Holy fuck!" Mere said.

"Try to breathe through the urge to push, Meredith. It's a fifteen-minute ride in the ambulance to Goodville. No offense, Josh, but I'd rather have a more sterile environment to deliver a baby."

"None taken," I replied honestly.

Meredith let out an ungodly shriek and gripped my hands hard enough to break them as Chaz rushed back into the room. Chaz screeched to a halt because he had a bird's-eye view of Trent kneeling in God only knew what on the floor between Meredith's legs. He nearly got knocked over when Tucker Garrison barreled into him.

"I heard the call come over my radio," Tucker said.

"Hey, Tuck," Meredith said. "I feel a burning sensation, but I can't say that I'm on fire."

"She still has her sense of humor," Tucker said as he maneuvered around Chaz and squatted down beside Trent. "I'm a trained medic for the fire department, honey. I've delivered babies a few times. The ambulance is on the way. I can hear the sirens, but they won't make it in time."

"Nope," Trent agreed. Then he and Tucker started trading medical jargon like on the television shows. Tucker got up, and Chaz joined him to help round up the things Trent needed.

"It burns so bad," Mere cried. "I didn't even have any warning. I had more Braxton Hicks than normal, and my back ached more than usual."

"Those probably weren't Braxton Hicks, and it sounds like you've been having back labor pains. It's not uncommon," Trent said. "The amniotic fluid acted as a cushion, so you weren't aware you've been in labor all this time."

"I'm so sorry, Mere," I said, kissing her temple. "I know this wasn't how you wanted to bring your little darling into the world."

"You're here, and that helps."

"I'm here too," Chaz said when he and Tucker returned. He shut the door to give her privacy then came around the table so he could hold Mere's hand. "We'll get through this together."

Mere let out an agonized cry and her body tensed in my embrace. "Oh my God! She's coming!"

"Head is clear," Trent said in a calm but urgent voice.

Meredith let out another long groan then went slack against me just as Trent said, "It's a baby girl." The most beautiful sound in the world is a newborn baby crying after taking their first breath.

"She's a beauty, Mama. I'm going to guess around eight and a half pounds."

Tucker handed Trent something that looked like a clamp and a pair of scissors he removed from a sterile bag. Then they carefully cleaned our baby girl with one towel and snuggly wrapped her up in another before handing her to Meredith.

"Hello, sweet angel," Meredith cooed. "I've been dreaming about you for so long. I must say, the reality is even more precious than the dream of you."

The kitchenette door burst open, and EMTs rushed in with the gurney. Gabe was on their heels but shielded his eyes so he wouldn't see anything Meredith didn't want him to see.

"Everyone okay in here?" he asked in his authoritative voice that always made my dick hard.

"Victoria and I are doing great," Meredith said.

Trent cleaned up in the sink while the paramedics positioned Meredith and her baby on the gurney for transportation. "I'm riding along too," he told the paramedics. "Just as a precaution," he assured Meredith when she looked concerned.

"Hey there, Tori," Gabe said, brushing a finger against her downy cheek. "I'm going to pick up your grandma, and we'll meet you at the hospital. Does Harley know?"

"He's on his way to Goodville," Chaz said. "Deanna picked up Mark and Daniel and will call John. I think she's heading to the hospital too."

"Adrian went to pick up Sally and the kids."

"I love you all so much," Meredith said tearfully. "Does Mama know you're coming to get her?"

"She commanded I come pick her up and said I better bring a car equipped with sirens and flashing lights. It was all I could do to get her to wait for me instead of rushing over here."

"I hate that she missed Tori's birth," Meredith said. "She won't get another chance either because I'm done!"

"I think every woman says that," Trent told her.

"At least the mothers of the children I've delivered," Tucker agreed. He extended his hand toward Trent. "I've seen you around town, but I've never introduced myself. I'm Tucker Garrison."

"Trent Love. It's good to meet you." I admit I was impressed he left off his official title, but it would seem a bit overkill at this point. It seemed like Trent finally learned the arts of subtlety and humility.

"Dr. Love?" Tucker asked. A sly grin spread across his face.

"I never thought about how my name would sound to people when I decided to go to medical school. I could retire already if I had a penny for every time someone made a joke about Dr. Love making house calls."

"You chose your career wisely. Oh, you probably want your hand back," Tucker said when he realized he still held Trent's hand. I could see the electricity arcing between them.

"Glad you were here," Gabe said when the men separated hands. He also extended his hand to Trent who accepted with a good-natured grin. Gabe then rolled his eyes when he caught Mere, Chaz, and me gawping at him in stunned silence.

"Glad I could help."

"We're ready for transport," one of the EMTs said.

"We'll see you real soon," I told Mere.

"Are they okay?" Dare asked once the coast was clear. He had a mop in one hand and bucket in the other. "I've already rescheduled your afternoon appointments."

"I'm going to miss your thoughtfulness and efficiency among many things when you're gone," I told him.

"I haven't left yet," Dare reminded me.

"It's only a matter of time before your design business takes off," I assured him. "You will be missed around here."

"Thanks, Josh."

"Ready to pick up Mama Richmond, Sunshine?" Gabe asked.

"Go on," Dare assured me. "I'll clean this up."

"I'll help," Tucker said. "I have industrial strength cleaner to sanitize the area."

"Thanks, Tuck," I told him. "I'm giving you free haircuts for a year for what you did today." I would do the same for Trent.

"It's not necessary, Josh."

"See what happens if you try to pay me," I warned.

Tuck held his hands up in surrender. "I'm still giving you a tip."

"I wouldn't if I were you," Gabe told him. "Just accept his gratitude, Tuck. It will go so much easier on you."

Gabe and I headed to his SUV after the ambulance left with Chaz following behind it. When we turned onto Mama Richmond's street, she was waiting for us at the curb.

"It's about damned time," she said when I opened the front passenger door to get out so she could ride up front with Gabe. "Better hurry your skinny ass up and get in the back seat, or we'll leave you behind. I can't believe I missed it. Tell me everything."

"Her water broke and Mere said, 'Oh. Ohhhh. Baby's coming.' And then she was just here. The whole labor and delivery couldn't have lasted more than a few minutes."

"Was she beautiful?" Mama Richmond asked Gabe.

"Breathtakingly beautiful," Gabe replied. "I forgot how soft babies' cheeks are, and it's giving me ideas." I met his eyes when he glanced into the rearview mirror. "She has so much hair, Mama."

Gabe's comment reminded me of one of the funniest moments of my life. I laughed so hard I had to clutch my belly. When I could finally catch my breath long enough to speak, I told them about Trent's comment and how we misunderstood what he meant.

Mama Richmond laughed until she cried. "I'm never going to let her live it down," she said, wiping her eyes.

"'You try lawn maintenance with a baby belly in the way.' You're priceless, Sunshine," Gabe said. "I bet Trent was embarrassed."

"Everything happened too fast for him to be embarrassed,

but I bet it changes once the adrenaline rush fades." I hoped I was around to see the look on his face.

Per Mama's request, Gabe got us to the hospital fast with the sirens blaring and lights flashing. I had to admit it was fun, especially when Chaz had to pull over so we could go around him. I was pretty sure he extended his middle finger as we drove by. I'd only been in the back of a police cruiser once, and they didn't turn on the lights when they hauled me to jail for getting into a fight on Black Friday.

"Where are they?" Mama asked Trent who stood just inside the emergency room doors.

"They took them up to the maternity floor to tend to Meredith and Victoria. You guys can head on up. I'll wait down here for everyone else."

Mama Richmond wrapped Trent up in a tight hug. "Thank you so much for helping my baby girl. God knew what he was doing when he placed you in her path today."

"It was my pleasure," Trent said. "I'm looking forward to seeing baby Tori grow up to be as bright and beautiful as her mama and grandmama."

"You're smooth," Mama said, pulling back. "Lucky for you I have a granddaughter to meet, or else, I'd be trying to find you a husband."

Trent chuckled and shook his head like he was unsure what to say. "I'll be up to check on my newest patient in just a few minutes. Dr. Pierce is up there with her now."

Mama Richmond power walked to the elevators without another word, leaving Gabe and me to scramble after her. The entire gang trickled in while we waited to see Meredith and Victoria. Poor Harley got stuck on the interstate and was the last to arrive. He passed through the gauntlet of hugs and happy tears as he made his way toward the information desk so he could ask to see his wife and daughter. Trent came out of the double doors wearing surgical scrubs before Harley had a chance to ask.

"Meredith sent me out to find you and Mama," Trent told him. He looked at the rest of us. "You guys can start cycling back in a little bit."

"Out of my way," Mama said, elbowing her way through the crowd. "I got fingers and toes to count. I heard my Tori has a head full of hair, and I want to see every curl. And then you people can have a turn." Mama cackled and followed Harley through the door.

Trent's face flushed a bright red, and I knew he remembered the conversation that took place in the salon kitchenette. I thought about entertaining our friends with the story while we waited but decided against it. It wasn't my story to tell, and I owed Trent a favor.

"You're not going to invite him to Sunday dinners now, are you?" Gabe asked from beside me. "I'm grateful for his actions today, but sharing a table with him is stretching my generosity."

"Maybe just the first one Meredith, Harley, and Tori attend after they come home." An idea occurred to me. I was pretty sure I saw a spark of interest when Trent shook Tuck's hand. "In fact, I think I'll invite Tucker to thank him also."

Gabe smirked because he knew what I was up to. "Just one dinner after we return from our vacation," he conceded.

"Deal," I said. "Now, what was it you said in the SUV about getting ideas?"

TWO

Gabe

"THIS ISN'T THE CAR I RENTED," I SAID TO THE AGENT AT THE front desk. "I requested a convertible Mini Cooper and was assured you would have one for me to pick up today. This," I gestured to the Volkswagen Beetle, "is neither a Mini Cooper nor a convertible."

"I'm sorry, Mr. Roman-Wyatt, there's obviously been a mistake. Another agent got the orders mixed up and gave your Mini to someone else this morning. I did call and ask them to return the car since they didn't pay for the upgrade, but they're halfway to Florida already."

I pinched the bridge of my nose and inhaled slowly through it, exhaling through my mouth. I'd never be the flexible pretzel Josh was, but I was learning yoga basics to help manage stress. "I understand mistakes are made, but I'd like to know how you're going to make this up to me?" The Beetle was cute, but there was no way in hell I was driving it all the way to the coast of South Carolina.

"I'm prepared to offer you an upgrade. We have a brand-new luxury vehicle with two moonroofs, top-of-the-line leather seats, and a killer stereo system. I'm willing to let you drive it at no additional cost to you."

"I'll take it," I said proudly. I had hoped to surprise Josh with a convertible Mini for this trip, but he wouldn't turn up his nose at a luxury car. My mind was spinning with all the possibilities as I waited for them to bring the car around. Cadillac? BMW? Audi? I glanced up as a shiny, black minivan pulled up to the door and stopped. I felt sorry for the poor sucker who had to drive it. I don't care how convenient it would be; a minivan was never going to be in my future.

The young employee who drove the car around the building entered the lobby and made a beeline straight for me. Maybe I needed to spend more time in the weight room if the guy looked at me and instantly thought soccer dad. I'd set him straight as soon as he tried to hand those keys off to me. "Are you Mr. Roman-Wyatt?"

"I am," I acknowledged, expecting him to say my ride would be brought around next.

"Here are your keys," he said, holding them out to me. "Let me show you some of the unique features the Chrysler Pacifica has to offer you, sir."

"Hold up," I said firmly. "The agent," I turned and gestured to the counter which was conveniently unoccupied, "told me I was getting a luxury vehicle upgrade since your company gave the car I wanted to the wrong customer this morning."

"Yeah?" he asked. "That's a bummer. What did you choose?"

"A convertible Mini Cooper," I replied.

"A Mini?" He looked me up and down like it was the last car he expected me to rent.

"It was a surprise for my husband."

"Oh, well, I'm sorry we made a mistake, but I can assure you the Pacifica is the most luxurious minivan on the road."

"Both my mother and mother-in-law own one to drive our kids around in, so I'm very familiar with it."

"You're all set then," he said with a huge grin, dangling the keys in front of me.

"Thanks," I grudgingly said when I accepted the keys.

"Safe travels, sir," the guy said as I walked away. I offered a brief wave and headed out to the van. I just hoped the rest of my vacation surprises didn't blow up in my face.

I reluctantly admitted the leather seats were nicer than any I'd sat in before, and the stereo system was as incredible as the agent promised. Leave it to Chrysler to put Harman Kardon speakers in a fucking minivan. By the time I merged onto the interstate to head north, I was jamming to classic rock and admiring the smooth way the van handled. When I pulled into the driveway, I was completely relaxed and ready to enjoy the night with my family.

I envisioned early bedtime for the babies so I could kick off the vacation with a midnight skinny dip with their daddy. I wanted us to be as relaxed as possible before we set off without our kids in the morning. The longest we had ever spent apart from them was a long weekend. An entire week away might be too much to ask, but we needed couple time. Our children would benefit in the long run because alone time would make our marriage even stronger.

A pizza delivery vehicle pulled up behind the minivan, and a teenaged girl got out of it. "Hello, Captain Roman-Wyatt," she said cheerfully.

"Hello, Natalie. How are your parents?"

"Doing well, sir. Here are your three extra-large pizzas. The order and tip were already paid by credit card. Did you order the pizza this time, or was it the birds placing an order through Alexa again?"

"I just pulled in the driveway, so I have no idea," I replied honestly. It could go either way. Maybe Josh envisioned a totally different evening than I had. "Have a good night, Natalie. Drive safely." She gave me a brief salute before turning and heading back to her car.

"Honey, I'm home," I said when I walked through the front door. No sounds of running toddlers, a dog, or my man greeted me. "Must be poolside," I said to myself as I walked through the house. I stopped by the large aviary and looked at Savage and Sassy. "Did you order the pizzas?"

"Suck my cock!" Savage squawked. "Suck it really good." Fuck! He sounded like he was repeating Josh from the other night. The ornery shit didn't miss a fucking thing which is why I knew he saw one of the grandpas hide the Easter egg in the dining room and gloated when we didn't find it until weeks later when the odor gave the location away.

"You better watch it, Dirty Bird."

"Smeller's the feller," Sassy said as if she knew the incident I was thinking about. It was exactly what Savage said when I had asked about the horrific smell.

"You too, Dirty Lady."

Joyful laughter floated in the air, pulling my attention away from our ornery birds. I would follow the sounds of my husband and children to the end of the earth if need be, but luckily, I only had to go as far as the pool.

"Hello, family," I said, stopping by the edge of the pool.

"Papa! Papa!" my beautiful babies exclaimed from their little floaty devices. I could see them kicking their legs happily in the water. Both of them wore tiny sunglasses and hats to protect their faces. Even though the hottest part of the day was behind us, I knew Josh had lathered them in sunscreen just to be careful.

"O Captain! My Captain," Josh said. "Why don't you lose some of those clothes and join us."

"This seems like an awful lot of pizza for two adults and two toddlers. Did the birds order pizza, or do we have company coming over tonight?"

"I thought about having everyone over because I wanted to see Tori one more time before we left. I can't believe she's a week old already. Then I realized that I just wanted a quiet night with you, our babies, and our parents." I was glad to see we were on the same page but not surprised by it.

"Does that mean you ordered three extra-large pizzas for six adults and two toddlers?"

"Wasn't me," Josh replied. "I think it's time we consider un-plugging Alexa before our birds order something embarrassing or so outlandish it overdraws our bank account." I didn't think that would really happen because the birds only repeated what they'd heard us say. Right? The pizza order they placed would've been the one I used if we were having a pool party that night.

"You don't have to convince me. I think it's fucking creepy." I couldn't understand why everyone wanted to be plugged into technology all the damn time. I knew it made me sound like I was seventy-five years old, but it didn't feel natural to me.

"Put those pizza boxes down, strip down to your boxers, and get in here. You look like you could use a refreshing swim before we eat the pizza."

"You don't have to tell me twice," I replied, setting the boxes down on the huge, rectangular patio table.

"Um, I already did," Josh said, reminding me that he'd already told me to lose my clothes.

I adored the hungry look in his eyes when he watched me strip down. I jumped in and swam underwater until I reached my family. I tugged on the twins' toes then popped up in time to catch them squealing with delight before I planted a firm kiss on their daddy's smiling lips.

"Papa! Papa!" I never tired of hearing them call my name while reaching their chubby hands toward me.

"My precious angels," I said, dropping low in the water so I could kiss their foreheads and they could wrap their arms around my neck.

"Tu bo!" Dylan yelled.

"Tu bo!" Destiny repeated.

They loved to play tug boat. I started making ridiculous engine noises, that made them giddy, and swam backwards, tugging them along.

"Fas!" Dylan yelled. He was my daredevil that wanted to do everything faster. I dreaded the thought of him driving as a teenager. Josh once said to me that our son would need to learn one day not everything was meant to be done faster.

I tugged them around for a few minutes while Josh swam under water and tickled their toes. Of course, he used their distraction to brush up against my body every chance he got too, as if I wasn't aware of where he was every second.

"Grandpa's here," I heard my dad say from the patio. I looked up and found him looking down at my pile of clothes on the chaise lounge. My mom stood beside him wearing a smirk and holding a pile of towels for us to dry off.

"Ah, you're the most beautiful family God ever put on *her* green earth," Bertie said tearfully. Bill hooked an arm around her shoulders and kissed the top of her head.

"Tug those babies over here and let me dry them off," my mom said. "Then you guys can get dried off, and we can eat this pizza.

Why in the world did you order so much, Gabe? Your dad and Bill will be eating leftovers the entire week you're away."

"The birds did it!"

"Uh huh." Mom didn't buy it for a minute. She might witness it firsthand if we left Alexa plugged in while we were away.

Our moms took Destiny and Dylan inside to get dressed, but our dads remained outside to guard the pizza, so I couldn't give Josh a proper honey-I'm-home kiss until we were alone upstairs. Josh stepped back after a few minutes and put some space between us before my dick was fully activated into fuck mode.

"To be continued," he said with a playful wink.

Our evening was as peaceful and beautiful as I had hoped it would be, and I couldn't help feeling emotional when we read stories to Destiny and Dylan before placing them in their cribs. I would miss story time with them so damn much.

The rental car didn't come up until later when we took the trash down to the curb so it was ready for pickup in the morning. Josh looked at the van, and even I had to admit it looked sleek in the moonlight. He spun around and placed both hands on my face. "You remembered." I didn't, but I nodded as if I did. "You're going to let me live out my fantasy of fucking you in one of those captain's chairs." *Ding. Ding. Ding.* Yeah, he jogged my memory good.

I began walking him backward to the minivan while I reached for the fob to open the side door. "Something about reclining the seats as far as they would go then opening the moonroof so you could make love to me beneath the stars."

"That's the one," Josh agreed. "It just never felt right borrowing one of our moms' vans to do the deed in."

"You get inside the van and think dirty thoughts while I go inside to retrieve the lube."

"Might as well bring a big bottle we can stash inside. We're going to get all kinds of use out of this baby," Josh said, gliding his hand over the armrest of the captain's chair. "Hurry, Gabe."

I didn't waste another second and jogged back inside and up the stairs to retrieve the lube. I nearly knocked over my dad in the hallway on my way back to Josh. He raised a brow when he saw what I had in my hand.

"Atta boy, Gabe," he said, patting me on the shoulder.

"Thanks, Dad. Just don't look out the windows overlooking the driveway." Bill and Bertie's eyes would be safe from my romp with Josh because their room overlooked the side yard.

"Don't you worry, Son. I have plans to keep your mama busy." Years ago, I would've gagged, but now, I appreciated how much effort my parents put into their marriage. It took a lot of energy to keep the love alive, but it was so fucking worth it.

Josh was still dressed when I returned to the van because he'd left the sliding door open for me. I wasn't upset, taking off his clothes was a huge turn-on for me. I pushed the button just inside the door to close us in while Josh hit the button to open the moon-roofs above the back seats.

"Look at all those stars," Josh whispered.

"I'm ready to see the moon," I teased, reaching for his firm ass cheeks. "Too cheesy?" I asked.

"A tiny bit but I'll let it slide because I'm so excited about this trip."

"You are?" I asked, pulling his shirt over his head then doing the same with mine. "I thought you'd be hesitant to leave Dylan and Destiny."

"I'm going to miss them like crazy, but I'm going to soak up every second we have alone together," Josh told me as I worked his shorts and underwear down his toned legs. "I'm going to relish being able to enjoy your body anytime I want."

My dick was as hard as a spike before I was fully naked. I was always hard and eager to please when we were alone. I reclined the captain's chair expecting Josh to coat my cock and climb on, but he lowered himself between my knees and licked a path up the rigid length of my erection. He chuckled around the head of my cock when I moaned in delight.

"This was the best idea I've had in a long time." I didn't feel at all bad for accepting full credit for something that was pure luck on my part.

I lost the ability to think by the time Josh was done torturing me with his mouth. Of course, he seemed to have just as much fun making me squirm while slicking up my cock for his ride. "I think we need to kick off our road trip with the ride of your life."

"My Sunshine," I reverently whispered when he sank down on my length and began to move—slowly and seductively. I couldn't look away from the way the moonlight glowed on his skin or the look in his eyes as he loved me with every inch of his perfect body. "Kiss me."

Josh lowered his upper body and braced his hands on both sides of my headrest. He chose to stare into my eyes while he sped up his torture instead of kissing me as I asked.

"Kiss me," I pleaded, craving his lips and tongue just as much as any other part of him. "Please."

He saw how much I needed him and gave me what I was begging him for. His tongue twined slowly around mine at first but sped up when he rode me faster. His teasing kisses became hungry and demanding as he sought pleasure from my body and, in return, rocked my world as only he could. I could tell he was about to come apart in my arms, so I gripped his hips hard and thrust up inside him.

"Yes!" Josh cried out hoarsely. Pleasure moved hard and swift through him, leaving him quaking in my arms and robbing him of the ability to speak as he panted through his orgasm in shaky breaths.

Then his mouth was back on mine, capturing my ecstatic cries as I pulsed and released deep inside him. Instead of cleaning up right away with one of our shirts so we could go inside, I pulled Josh down onto my chest so I could extend the serenity I felt with him.

"This is one hell of a way to start off our vacation," Josh whispered sleepily.

"It will be one we never forget," I assured him as I felt sleep creeping up to claim me.

THREE

Josh

Falling asleep naked on Gabe's chest after a mind-blowing orgasm while he held onto my ass cheeks like I might try to flee in the night was nothing new. We usually woke up after a little catnap, cleaned ourselves up, put on pj pants, and went back to sleep. Waking up in the back of a minivan just before dawn was an entirely new experience.

"Oh shit," I said, suddenly jerking up to a sitting position.

It was followed by Gabe roaring, "Oh fuck!" when I yanked out several of his chest hairs that were stuck in my dried cum, gluing us together.

"I'm so sorry," I said, running my hand soothingly over his stinging flesh. "I just realized we've been in this minivan all night long. We need to get dressed and sneak back inside the house before the neighborhood wakes up."

Gabe jackknifed up in the chair so fast he nearly headbutted me. "Ow," he said, rubbing his lower back. "These seats are comfortable, but they aren't made for sleeping in for long hours. Or maybe I'm just starting to feel my age."

"You're not even forty yet," I replied with a quirked brow. "I would say it's the awkward position and the one hundred and fifty pounds of dead weight that slept on your chest."

Through it all, Gabe had maintained his grip on my ass. He gave me an extra squeeze. "It's probably why I slept so well."

A noise to our left had us both looking out the long window. Our paper girl, Amanda, rode up beside the van and launched our paper onto the porch. Gabe and I froze in place and didn't say a word, hoping she wouldn't hear us. The windows were tinted, so I had high hopes she wouldn't see us. It was the last sort of scandal we needed in our lives. I don't think we breathed until she was out of sight.

"That was close," I whispered. "We need to dress and get in the house before Mr. Sanders across the street begins watering his flower beds.

"Good call."

We shut the moonroof and pulled on our clothes as quickly as we could before hustling up to the front porch. I was happy we were able to get to the house without being seen, but my relief died when Gabe tried to open the door only to discover it was locked.

"Oh no."

"Use your keys," I said.

"I didn't bring my normal set of keys. I only have the ones for the rental van. I didn't think we'd get locked out of our own home," he whisper-shouted.

"One of the dads must have made the rounds and locked the door. Hey, I know. Use the spare key we keep hidden beneath the flower pot. Oh, wait. You won't let me hide a spare key."

"Because I don't want people trying to murder us in our sleep," Gabe countered. "Can you wait and bust my balls *after* we find our way back inside?"

Every day with this man made me love him more and more. It didn't matter if we were talking, fucking, playing with our kids, or arguing; I couldn't imagine a day where I'd look at him and think *meh*. "You know what we need to do, right? We have to suck it up and ring the doorbell or drive off and buy everything we need for our vacation."

Gabe snorted. "Like either one of us is leaving without kissing our children goodbye."

"True. You want me to climb the downspout up to the second story and try to climb in our bedroom?"

"I wouldn't attempt it with the way this vacation is starting out," Gabe replied.

I tipped my head to the side because he was correct. I was about to agree with him when the front door suddenly opened. Al looked at us with wide eyes and a knowing grin.

"You fellas camp out in the swanky van?" he teased.

"Not on purpose, Dad," I told him. "We fell asleep and realized we didn't have our house keys when we tried to sneak back in."

"Life surely is an adventure for the two of you," Al said, stepping aside so we could enter. "Your mama is up in Destiny and Dylan's room getting them dressed for the day."

"Race you," Gabe said then took off before I could accept or decline his challenge. Gabe's body had suffered the brunt of the abuse overnight, so he was no match for me. I reached the nursery before Martina had freed either one of them from their cribs.

"Good morning," Martina said, eyeing our wrinkled clothing and haggard expressions. "You boys been out carousing all night long?"

"Sort of," I replied sheepishly. "Do you mind if we get the munchkins ready and meet you downstairs?"

"Of course not," she said. Then she hugged me tight and kissed my cheek. "I know what a worrier you are, but we have everything covered. You go have an amazing time with your husband. I know it's hard to leave the kids behind, but believe me when I tell you the break is healthy for both daddies and babies. I promise we'll stick to your dietary guidelines."

"Oh no," I said. "Am I that bad?"

"Not at all. There's nothing wrong with wanting to keep additives and preservatives out of their diets and feeding them organic meats that are free of hormones and antibiotics. You've changed the way I look at food. For the better," she added in case I wasn't convinced.

"I still let them eat McNuggets on occasion," I said. It was a rite of passage after all.

"We'll make our own just like you do," Martina assured me. She then looked at her son. "Drive carefully, and don't forget to check in when you arrive. Tell Bonita and the girls I said hello."

"Bonita!" I said suddenly. "We're going to Tennessee to see Bonita and your sisters?"

"Oops," Martina said then dashed out of the room, leaving Gabe to answer me.

"We're passing through Tennessee on our way to our final destination," Gabe grudgingly answered. "They're meeting us for lunch, so we better get a move on."

"At least I know we're heading south," I said smugly. "I bet you're taking me to some beach resort in Florida so we can be lazy in the sun for a week."

"Not even close," Gabe replied. "You'll never guess, so save your energy. Help me get these rascals ready then we can give them proper kisses goodbye and get on the road."

"What about breakfast?" I asked.

"We'll stop for a bite after we hit the road."

"It's a good thing I already packed our bags in advance," I told Gabe. I picked my little princess up and kissed her cheeks until she squealed in delight. After they had clean butts and clothes on, I traded Gabe so I could give my prince's cheeks equal smooches. How the hell was I supposed to survive an entire week without kissing their faces? It would be hard, but I was eager to have Gabe all to myself.

"I'll pass the babies off to the grandparents while you start the shower."

"Coffee, please."

"Of course," I replied. Hardly a morning went by when I didn't hand Gabe a cup of coffee while he was in the shower. Of course, that was usually followed by mutual blow jobs, but we were already behind schedule, so I settled for toe-curling kisses instead.

"God, whose life is this?" I whispered in between kisses.

"Ours," he answered. "Just enjoy it, Sunshine."

Once we were dressed and ready, I pointed to the suitcases in the corner of our bedroom. "I might have overpacked."

"You think?" Gabe asked, rubbing his neck while checking out the four suitcases.

"I wasn't sure what we would need, but that single suitcase you packed surely wasn't enough."

"Well, we have the room, and who knows where this adventure will take us? Ready to kiss the babies and our parents goodbye and get on the road?"

"Yep," I said enthusiastically. "I'm ready."

I didn't cry or cling to the babies after we said our goodbyes. I didn't repeat their daily routines to grandparents who knew them as well as I did. I reached for my husband's hand and allowed him to take me away on a surprise vacation.

"You're handling this better than I thought you would," Gabe said once we backed out of the driveway.

"Leaving the babies with four grandparents who love them?" I asked.

"Blindly following me wherever I want to go."

"I am a bit of a control freak," I said, earning a chuckle from Gabe. "I don't mind following when I trust the leader. There's no one on this planet I trust more than you."

Gabe reached over the console and linked our fingers together. "I will make sure it's always the case, Sunshine."

We stopped at Tim Horton's for coffee and bagels just before we reached the Kentucky border. Gabe ordered a toasted everything bagel with garden vegetable cream cheese, and I got a double toasted twelve-grain bagel with cream cheese and a thin layer of strawberry jam on top of it.

"Why not just get strawberry cream cheese?" Gabe asked once we returned to the van.

"It's not the same thing at all," I countered.

"It's cream cheese and strawberry jam put separately rather than a cream cheese that already has strawberries mixed with it," Gabe pointed out. "I hardly see the difference." So, I held my bagel to his mouth and let him take a bite to see for himself. "Okay, it's not the same thing at all. Do you want to trade? You're the health nut."

"No, I don't want to trade," I scoffed. "I would've ordered the everything bagel with veggie cream cheese if it was what I wanted."

"Half and half?" Gabe pleaded, turning on those puppy dog eyes.

"Fine, but you're getting the half you already took a chomp out of. Don't think you're getting a half plus a chomp."

I quietly ate while Gave drove us back toward the southbound interstate ramp. One of my favorite things about us as a couple was our comfortable silences. Neither of us felt the need to fill every second with chatter. I hummed and sang out of tune along with the music while Gabe grinned because he was happy there was something I couldn't do well.

"Have you decided against opening a second location in Cincinnati?" Gabe asked. "You didn't seem thrilled with the idea." I received a proposal from a prosperous businessman who'd become a fan of my show. He'd researched the success and growth of my salon and assumed I was looking to expand. I wasn't.

"A few years ago, I might've jumped all over it, but not now."

"Why? What's different?"

"There are only so many hours in a day, and I don't want to waste them on the road. I built a business and a life in my hometown, and it's where I plan to stay until I die."

"It's not because you feel like the kids and I hold you back, right?"

I nearly wrenched my neck when I turned my head suddenly in his direction. "You're not serious, are you?" He couldn't be serious.

"Of course, I'm serious. I don't want to be the reason you don't experience life to the fullest."

"Babe, my cup runneth over. The only expansion I want to work on is our family. In another year or so," I rushed to add.

"Another year," Gabe whined. "Is it a hard line in the sand?"

"What are you thinking?" I asked.

"Next few months. As soon as possible."

"Don't you think we should get the ankle biters we have potty trained before we bring home a new baby?"

"Probably," Gabe hesitantly agreed. "This is all Mere's fault for bringing Tori over every day. I miss the new baby smell."

"Oh my God! You sound like me after the new car smell wears off."

"I'm serious," Gabe said softly. "I want more children."

"I want more children too."

"How many more?" Gabe asked suddenly.

"I was thinking one, two at the most."

"Two at the same time or one now and another down the road?" he asked.

"One set of twins is enough," I told him. "I vote for one at a time."

"Sounds like a plan," Gabe agreed. "I still think we need to get the paperwork started."

"Okay, but I'm warning you now. We're going to get a phone call a week later. Be ready for more diapers than we can keep up with and sleepless nights."

"I'll be ready," Gabe said excitedly. "Now that I'm getting a new baby as soon as possible, let's get back to the salon business discussion. Are you sure you don't want to expand the salon and hire a staff for the Cincinnati location? You wouldn't need to work there yourself."

"How will I know if they're operating up to my standards if I'm never there? I can't put my name on something then neglect it. I think I've found a solution to make all parties involved happy."

"Yeah, and what would your plan be?"

"I would offer my consultation services to help Rhett Bartlet choose and train the staff, design the salon, and implement the processes and ideals that make Curl Up and Dye so successful while keeping in mind an urban salon will have different needs than a rural one. I'll do this for a fee, of course."

"Certainly," Gabe agreed. "It sounds like a big commitment."

"It would be initially, but I walk away free and clear once the salon is up and running."

"I think it sounds like a wonderful idea."

"I have contacts at all the cosmetology schools, so I have access to all the best stylists. Josi's cousin lives in Cincinnati and currently manages a salon. I bet I can pull him over to our side."

"It won't be your side though," Gabe reminded me. "Do you want Josi's cousin to make the leap if you're not there to ensure it's a good environment?"

"That's an excellent point. I wouldn't ask him to uproot himself unless he's unhappy at his current job."

"You think Rhett will go for it?"

"It's no skin off my nose if he doesn't. This wasn't an opportunity I sought, so I don't have anything invested or anything to lose."

"I can see why your salon is so damn successful," Gabe said. "You have the perfect trifecta working for you—talent, business smarts, and people skills."

"Thanks, babe."

"I'm just telling it how I see it." Gabe glanced over at the clock. "We've been on the road for more than an hour, and you haven't asked me one time where we're going."

"I told you, Gabe. I trust you." And maybe I accidentally saw the charge for the gorgeous inn located near the coast of South Carolina on the credit card statement. It would be my little secret because I didn't want to spoil his fun.

FOUR

Gabe

"Here we are," I said, pulling into Bonita and Miguel's driveway. I was excited to see my biological mother, her husband, and my three half sisters. "I'm happy to stretch my legs for a bit."

"Me too," Josh said. "I'm also excited to eat whatever Bonita made for lunch."

We didn't have to ring the doorbell to announce our arrival because my youngest sister, Arianna, opened the door as soon as we stepped onto the front porch. "Gabe!" she exclaimed then launched herself into my open arms. "I've missed you."

Arianna, Selena, and Marisol drove north to Blissville after their schools let out and stayed for two weeks, so it had only been a little over a month since we last saw them. Of course, I understood where she was coming from since we'd only known about each other for a few years. There was always so much sadness when I realized how much of their lives I missed out on. Calling, skyping, and texting could only get us so far because nothing compared to being physically in the same place.

"Quit hogging our brother," Marisol said, stepping onto the porch.

Arianna turned loose of me so she could launch herself at Josh at the same time I caught Marisol. "I have the most handsome two brothers on the planet," she squealed. "Not to mention the most precious niece and nephew to ever live."

"All of you are still coming up for a visit next month, right?" I asked.

"We wouldn't miss it," Bonita said, joining the fray. "How are you, Gabriel?"

"I'm great, Bonita. I'm excited to see all of you and spend some alone time with my husband this week." I noticed my oldest sister was nowhere in sight which was odd. "Where's Selena?" I asked.

"She's hiding inside," Marisol mock whispered.

"Hiding? From me?" I asked with concern. It wasn't like Selena. "Have I said something to upset her?" She didn't sound upset on the phone last week. In fact, I'd never heard her sound so happy. Why the sudden... Oh. Someone special to her was responsible for the extra exuberance she'd displayed during our conversation. Someone she was worried about introducing to me. "Is he a decent guy?" I asked Bonita. I didn't want to go in there with guns blazing and scare away someone she cared about if he treated my sister with the respect she deserved.

"He's a great guy," Bonita said. The tone of her voice added a silent *but* at the end.

"Then why the hesitation?" I asked, feeling my brow furrow into the deep V Josh said would cause me to wrinkle prematurely.

"He's older than you," Arianna said.

"Excuse me?" I asked. "How much older?"

"He's already forty," Marisol replied dramatically.

"Forty?" I asked. "Selena is only twenty-five."

"We know," Arianna said drily.

"Babe," Josh said softly, placing his hand between my shoulder blades. "Let's try to remember Selena is a brilliant young lady who's capable of deciding what is best for her."

"He's right," Selena said confidently as she stepped onto the porch. I noticed she didn't have her new guy with her. "Can we talk alone for a few minutes?" Everyone besides Selena and I went inside the house. I guess it was their answer to her question. "Sit with me?" she asked, gesturing to the porch swing.

I followed her without saying anything. I wasn't sure what to say, and I thought it was best to let her lead the conversation. We sat quietly for a minute or two, just gently swinging on the porch while she chose her words and I urged myself not to act like a crazy, overprotective brother.

"I should've told you this over the phone last week," Selena finally said, breaking the silence. "It would've given you time to process the news."

"Why didn't you?" I asked curiously.

"It also would've allowed you to run a background check on Charlie," she teased.

"That's a bad thing?"

"Only if you don't trust me," Selena countered.

"Sis, there are situations where I am going to trust you and your intentions while doubting those around you. It doesn't mean I trust you less. It just means I'm proceeding with caution."

"And you think this is one of those times? All you know about

Charlie is his age, and you're ready to doubt him. It seems a little jaded, big brother."

"Life has taught me to be cautious with those I love, Selena. Never doubt for a second I love you, but you've got to give me a little bit of a break here. I didn't even know you were seeing anyone, and they sprung it on me before I get inside the house."

"I know you love me, and it's why we're having a mature conversation."

"Can I ask you a question?"

"Sure," she said, tilting her head so she could look up at me.

"Are you happy?"

"Deliriously so," she admitted. A sly smile crept across her face. "Charlie had a big problem with the age difference when he found out he was fifteen years older than I was, but it never bothered me. He started avoiding me and making excuses why he couldn't meet me for coffee or a drink. Charlie wanted me to date someone closer my age, but I've never liked guys my age. They're too immature."

"I can see where that would be an issue for you," I admitted. "Are you guys on the same page about what you see five, ten, and fifteen years down the road?"

"You're getting a little ahead of yourself there, Gabe. We haven't been dating for very long."

"It doesn't always matter. Just answer me this: will this guy do everything in his power to make sure your dreams of becoming a doctor are realized?"

"I will," a deep voice said. I glanced up and saw Charlie had come to see what was holding us up. I admired his bravery.

"Charlie Higgins," he said, approaching me with and outstretched hand.

"Gabriel Roman-Wyatt," I said, gripping his hand firmly.

"My ears were burning," Charlie teased. "As independent and fierce as she is, I didn't feel right about leaving Selena out here to face the music so to speak."

"I'm not angry; I'm surprised," I assured him. I had many questions flying through my mind, but none of them were my business. Only one thing mattered, and I decided to lay it on the line for him. "You and I won't have any problems as long as you treat my sister with the care and respect she deserves."

"I promise."

The three of us went inside the house to find everyone else.

"Poolside," Selena said. "Mama prepared a feast, and I believe she asked Daddy to set up the tables on the veranda so we could enjoy the nice weather. It's been so humid lately, so we're enjoying the break for however long it lasts."

Josh glanced up from sipping a margarita when I walked onto the veranda. "Hey, I'm not driving."

I dropped down in the chair beside him and accepted the glass of lemonade he extended to me. I kissed his smiling lips before I quenched my thirst.

Bonita set up a delicious, buffet-style feast. I didn't put as much on my plate as I wanted because I knew the combination of filling food and warm air would make me sleepy, and I had several more hours of driving left. I kept my portions small so I could sample a little bit of everything and not stuff myself as I did on Thanksgiving.

We kept the conversation light and caught up with what was going on in everyone's lives. Charlie seemed like a good guy and appeared to care about Selena and her dreams. Bonita, Miguel, and my other sisters seemed to like him just fine, so who the hell was I to give them grief? I'd save my chest-thumping for a time when I felt it was warranted.

After lunch, everyone walked us to our van to see us off. Hugs and handshakes were exchanged then Josh gave Bonita several recent pictures of the twins. She held them against her chest after silently staring at them for several minutes. "I can't wait to see Destiny and Dylan again," she said with tears in her voice. "I'm so excited to be a part of their lives. You don't know how much it means to me. Thank you."

"We love you," Josh said. "Of course, we want you in their lives. Besides, without you, I wouldn't have Gabe and the kids. I would have a hole in my universe I could never fill. I thank you and your act of love every day, Bonita."

"Oh, you always say the sweetest things," Bonita said then sniffled as she wiped away her tears. "You guys drive carefully. Let me know if you want to stop by on your way home, and I'll gladly feed you again."

"Be careful what you wish for," I warned before hugging her one last time. "I'll text you when we arrive so you won't worry."

"Thank you, Gabe."

The interior of the van was stifling hot when we got back inside it. Josh adjusted the temperature controls, and I rolled down the windows until the air coming out of the vents was cool. Once I backed out of the driveway, I honked and returned everyone's waves as we drove down the street.

"I wish we could've stayed longer," Josh said. "I feel like we ate and ran."

"We did, but Bonita knew to expect it since we have a lot of driving left."

"Bonita knows where we're going, but I don't?" Josh asked.

"She knows the state and number of hours left on our drive, not where we'll be staying or what we'll be doing."

Josh snorted. "I bet she can guess what we'll be doing."

"I'm going to bet Bonita doesn't allow her mind to go there," I countered.

"You handled the thing with Charlie well, Gabe. I'm impressed."

"Thank you," I said as a suspicious thought wormed its way into my brain. "You didn't seem very surprised."

"I wasn't," Josh replied casually. "I've known about Charlie for a while now." I don't know why his admission felt like an act of betrayal, but right or wrong, that's how it felt. "It wasn't my place to

36

tell you, babe." He accurately read my mind, or maybe it was my tense body language. "Besides, you would know these things if you ever engaged on social media."

"Devil's creation," I replied. I would never get over my dislike of social media. Up until that moment, I had expected Josh to stay relevant with those types of things and keep me updated. I realized my game plan wasn't going to work.

Josh chuckled. "I know exactly what you're thinking."

"You can't possibly."

"You're wondering how you can trust me to tell you important things when our kids are older."

"I was not."

"You were, and I'll explain to you why you'll be able to trust me. Are you ready?" He didn't wait for me to answer him before continuing. "The most obvious reason is your sister is an intelligent, free-thinking woman who is in love for the first time in her life. No, she didn't tell me about Charlie. It's what I observed with my own eyes when I saw the pictures she posted on the devil's creation. You saw the smile on her face today, right?"

"Yes."

"It's only a fraction of what I've seen in the pictures. It was her place to tell you, not mine. I don't feel the same way when it comes to our kids, because we're equal partners in their lives. I would never keep secrets about our children from you. Dylan and Destiny will know it as soon as they're old enough to understand."

"I couldn't ask for anything more," I replied honestly. "I can promise you the same respect too."

Josh leaned over the console and kissed my cheek. "Selena will be just fine, Gabe. I can tell these things."

I wasn't sure how Josh and I would handle a long road trip together. Even though we went together like peas and carrots, our personalities, especially our choice of entertainment, were vastly different. We took turns choosing music, and I flipped over to a sports talk show when Josh decided he wanted to read a beta copy of Chaz's upcoming book release. I had no idea what a beta copy was, but he was excited, and I got to find out the latest sports gossip.

It didn't take me long to get caught up on the trade rumors in the NBA, how the NFL rookies were doing in camps, and world series predictions. Nothing I learned was all that surprising, but I loved the way the different hosts approached each topic. Sometimes, they all agreed, and other times, they argued like Dylan and Destiny over a toy. I glanced over at Josh to see if the back-and-forth bickering was bothering him, but he was too absorbed in his book to notice.

I chuckled at the way he bit his bottom lip like he did when something was getting suspenseful in a movie or television show. I'd read enough of Chaz's books to know he liked to shake things up a bit, so I figured he must've leaned more toward a thriller than a romance with the new book. A few seconds later, I saw Josh reach up and fiddle with the collar of his T-shirt out of the corner of my eye. Biting lips and fidgeting with clothes made me think he was reading something sexy instead of scary. It wasn't a minute later before he started squirming in his seat a little.

I reached over and gently squeezed his thigh. "It must be a hot book."

Josh loudly gasped and dropped his Kindle on the floorboard between his feet. "Jesus!" he exclaimed. "You scared the fuck out of me."

"Don't say Jesus and fuck in the same sentence," I chastised.

"*I* didn't, but *you* just did. I put an exclamation mark after Jesus and started a new sentence."

Okay, maybe he had me there. "What made you so jumpy?"

"This is Chaz's best book to date. It's suspenseful, sexy, and a little taboo."

"Taboo?" I asked.

"Taboo-ish."

"What does that even mean?" I guess anyone could apply the word taboo to just about any situation.

"Well, the main characters aren't blood-related," Josh said. "The state they live in would recognize them as brothers, however."

"Whoa."

"It's not nearly as tawdry as I just made it sound," Josh rushed to tell me. "Their parents met and married when they were little kids. Their bond was instantaneous and innocent, but over time…"

"It became less innocent?"

Josh nodded. "There's so much more to it though. The older brother—for lack of a better word—joined the military to get away from the younger brother. He wanted to resist temptation and do right by him which he thought he was doing by staying away. A series of events occur when he comes home on leave for a family emergency and grief breaks the tenuous control he's always had, and it sets off a chain reaction that will impact their lives and keep them separated for more than a decade. They've just reconnected, and I had to bite my lip from crying. It's beautiful."

I had to admit it sounded interesting.

"The heart wants what the heart wants," Josh softly said as he retrieved his book. This time, he placed his left hand palm up on the console, inviting me to hold his hand.

I returned my attention to sports talk, and Josh got lost in his fictional world again, but our joined hands kept us tethered to each other.

FIVE

Josh

PLAYING DUMB WAS HARDER TO DO THAN I EVER IMAGINED. WHEN we crossed over the North Carolina state line, I started guessing all the places we were going in the state. I knew damn well we were heading to Tarlington House located south of Charleston, South Carolina. Once I saw the name on the credit card statement, I couldn't resist looking into the history of the majestic home built in 1810. My God, the stories those walls could tell. As beautiful as I found the home to be, I wasn't excited about staying in a plantation home I assumed was built on the backs of slaves and overlooked fields worked by slaves. Then I read about the role the plantation played in the Underground Railroad system and was reminded not to rush to judgment and make assumptions.

Tarlington House was built by Jeffrey Tarlington, a union sympathizer who worked his land with only the help of his wife and eight children. They used the plantation's proximity to the river to help slaves escape, knowing they would be killed if anyone ever found out. Once I learned the facts, I couldn't wait to sleep under the same roof as such a brave family.

I wanted to wipe the smug grin off Gabe's face when my fake guesses fell short each time, but I wouldn't ruin the fun trip he planned with my need to always come out on top. I smiled mischievously because I had plenty of ideas about how I could come out on top once we arrived.

"What's up with the big smile?" Gabe asked suspiciously.

"I'm just happy to have this time with you."

"Yeah, I can tell it's a genuine reply, but I also know there's more to your smug smile. What do you have packed in those bags?"

"I didn't bring our sex swing if that's what you're asking."

Gabe snorted. "I was thinking smaller, more portable items."

"Well, since you assured me we wouldn't be going through airport security, I did bring along some fun things—both old and new."

"I didn't realize you meant sex toys when you said you were shopping for vacation," Gabe teased.

"I figured you would appreciate some surprises too."

"Every day is a surprise with you, Sunshine." Lucky for him, I heard the affection in his voice.

"How much further before we reach our destination?" I asked. "I need to use the bathroom."

"We have a few hours yet, but I'll need to stop for gas soon."

"You want me to use a bathroom at a gas station?" Did he even know me?

"I figured we'd find an exit that also has a few restaurants to choose from," Gabe replied. "You need clean bathrooms, and I need to recharge my batteries."

"Good deal," I agreed. "I could use a recharge for my batteries too."

"Something fast or something good?"

"Both," I answered. "Oh, there's a Popeyes chicken at the next exit. We have ourselves a winner."

After a quick fill-up at the gas station, Gabe drove to Popeyes. He ordered our food to go at the counter while I went to the bathroom. We traded places when I was through then we got back on the road.

"Babe, we could've eaten this inside the restaurant where you could enjoy it better."

"Nah, I'm hoping to time our arrival so you can see our vacation spot as the sun sets."

The drive to Charleston was supposed to take nine hours and fifty minutes in normal traffic but stopping for a visit at Bonita's added another hour to our travel time, and there was an accident on the interstate, causing a thirty-minute delay. I figured our almost ten-hour trip would take closer to twelve by the time we arrived at Tarlington House. It would put us there at about eight o'clock, giving us a bit of time to settle in and enjoy the sunset. I hoped Gabe was able to finagle one of the rooms off the gorgeous second-story balcony. I could easily picture drinking mojitos and watching the sun set from one of those rocking chairs I saw in the photos on the Tarlington House website. I had to hand it to my husband; he sure knew how to pick a vacation spot.

"Did you finish your book?" Gabe asked.

"Not yet. I want to devour every word, but I want to savor it at the same time."

"Like a scrumptious apple pie?"

"Yes, like a decadent dessert you never want to stop eating. I think I'll play a game on my iPad instead."

"What game?" Gabe asked.

"*Clue*. It's my favorite board game and now my favorite app."

"Why have we never played *Clue*?"

I snorted. "If you think I'm good at *Monopoly*, you should see me at *Clue*."

"I'm not surprised. Do you imitate Deputy Chief Brenda Leigh Johnson when you play?"

"Does your dick get hard when I spin on my pole?" I asked, making Gabe laugh.

"I'd like to make a prediction, y'all," Gabe said in a baby soft, Southern accent. "I think it was Miss Scarlett, in the library, with the candlestick. Thank you."

"You do a pretty mean Brenda Leigh, babe. Maybe it can be your next Halloween costume."

"It would be a vast improvement over our *Miami Vice* costumes," Gabe countered. "Please don't make me wear one of her ugly sweaters though. Pick one of the prettier outfits."

"You got it," I assured him. "Who should I dress as then?"

"Fritzy, of course," Gabe replied. He used the same voice Brenda used when she was trying to charm Fritz into doing something he didn't like and using a nickname he liked even less. His costume suggestion had a lot of merit.

"Oh, we're heading into South Carolina," I said excitedly. "You're taking me to Myrtle Beach. I haven't been there since I was a kid."

"Nope, but I will at least confirm our vacation destination is in the same state. You can go ahead and text our mothers with the update so it's not so obvious you want to find out how the babies are doing."

"They're probably giving the babies their baths and getting them ready for bed. I'll wait until we get there and get settled."

"Maybe we can FaceTime Dylan and Destiny in the morning. You don't think it will upset them too much, do you?"

"Dylan and Destiny are getting spoiled rotten every single second of each day we're away. This is much harder on us than it is on them," I told Gabe. "I did bring an extra copy of their favorite book so we could read a bedtime story to them."

"You think of everything," Gabe said. "No wonder you brought so many bags."

"I do like to be prepared," I agreed. Once I learned about our destination, I accidentally saw another surprise Gabe had in store for me because the event was listed on the website. Gabe said he had everything planned out, but I packed some extra things to be sure.

I worried I wouldn't be able to pull off shock and awe when we finally arrived, but my reaction when Gabe drove down the half-mile lane to Tarlington House was genuine. The pictures on the internet didn't do this place justice.

"I feel like we're driving through an enchanted forest," I told Gabe, as I looked at the dense woods on both sides of the drive. "Is there a castle at the end of this driveway?"

"No, but I think it's the next best thing," Gabe said as we pulled into the clearing and I got my first look at Tarlington House.

"Oh my God!" I exclaimed softly. "She's more beautiful than a castle. You chose well, babe." My eyes struggled to take in all her graceful beauty at once. The ivory, federal-style home and surrounding grounds were stunning. "Look at the second-story balcony. I bet the view is just amazing."

"That door is to the suite I rented for the week," he proudly said. "You'll have plenty of time to check out the view when you drink your coffee in the morning or make love to me at night."

"I bet we'll see a lot of stars tonight," I said, picturing the two of us cuddled beneath a blanket on our private porch.

A man in a suit came out the front door of Tarlington House

when Gabe rounded the curve in the driveway. There were two sets of steps leading up to the large porch. The gentleman jogged down the left set and approached our vehicle when Gabe came to a stop.

"Good evening, gentlemen. Are you checking in?"

"We are," Gabe said. "We have a reservation for Roman-Wyatt."

Another man jogged down the same set of steps and joined him. "I'm your concierge, José. You'll see me filling in many roles here at Tarlington House. Tonight, I'll also act as your valet. This," he clasped the second man, "is David, and he will make sure your luggage arrives at your room while you check in."

I suddenly felt terrible about the amount of luggage I packed. "David probably wants us to drag our owns suitcases around."

"Nah," David replied affably, "I'm prepared for everything. You leave it to me."

Gabe shrugged and opened his door to get out. "I'll return the keys to you in a jiffy," José told him.

Gabe reached for my hand, and together, we went inside to check in at the front desk while the guys took care of the van and luggage. The outside of the house was impressive, but the view when I first walked in blew me away.

"I've never seen a double, curving staircase," I said in awe.

"It was designed by the same architect who built the White House," said a warm voice to the right of us.

I looked over at the check-in counter and smiled at the woman patiently waiting for us to come over. "Everyone has the same jaw-dropping reaction when they come to Tarlington House for the first time."

Gabe placed his hand at the small of my back and guided me to the counter. "I'm Gabriel Roman-Wyatt, and this is my husband, Josh."

"It's lovely to meet you both. I hope you're looking forward to your stay."

She then handed us a folder and went into detail about all the activities and amenities they had to offer. I'd never gone horseback riding before, but no way was I leaving without riding one through the woods, preferably guided by someone who knew what they were doing and where they were going. The jet skis and canoeing outings also sounded fun. I expected Gabe to react one way or the other, but he kept staring at the woman who introduced herself as Geneva Louderback. The entire time she spoke, Gabe was watching her with an expression I could only describe as adoration.

"Excuse me," he finally said. "I hope you won't think me inappropriate, but I just want to say how much I admire your son, not only for his athleticism but the kind of man he is off the court."

Geneva placed her hand over her heart and smiled even broader. "I don't think it's inappropriate at all. I think it's wonderful to hear. I am so proud of my boy."

"As you should be."

"Your room is located on the second floor. You have the balcony room at the front. If you don't want to take the staircase, the elevator is—"

"We'll use the glorious staircase, Geneva," I told her.

"It's a beauty," she said. "Here are your room keys. Dinner was served a few hours ago, but we do offer room service if you're hungry. There's a menu in your room, but feel free to call down if you need anything or have questions."

"Thank you," I said, looping my arm through Gabe's. "I have a feeling it will be a vacation we will never forget."

"That's our aim," she said with a genuine smile. "David will bring your luggage up to you in just a bit. I'll have him bring your car keys up too."

We thanked her once more then made our way up the grand staircase. Of course, I took the left stairs when Gabe headed for the right. Had it been our house, I would've raced him to the top, but I was trying to show I was a sophisticated man. I was doing good until Gabe opened the double doors with one of the nifty, antique-looking skeleton keys Geneva gave him.

"Fuck. Me." My mouth gaped open as I looked around the suite. The four-poster bed was either one hell of a replica piece or a genuine antique. The intricately carved details on the headboard, footboard, and posts were stunning. Through an open door, I could see a huge claw foot tub, and I planned to take full advantage of it as soon as possible. The sitting room on the opposite side of the bedroom area was spacious and filled with comfortable furniture.

"This reminds me of our suite at home," I told Gabe when I could find my voice.

"We're only missing the balcony. Are you ready to check it out?"

We opened the double doors, and it was like we were stepping into another world. The balcony overlooked the driveway, but beyond it, all I could see were beautiful trees. The sun was dropping lower in the sky as Gabe pulled me into his arms and kissed me long and slow.

"I've been thinking of this moment ever since I booked our stay."

"Yeah?" I asked. "What else have you been thinking about?"

"Knock knock," David said from the open doorway. He pushed a luggage cart into the room and immediately proceeded to unload it.

"Here, let me help," Gabe said, rushing to his side. "My husband gets a little carried away." Oh yes, I planned to get carried away as soon as we were alone again.

"Trust me, guys. This is nothing compared to what I'll be unloading later in the week."

"Thank you, David," Gabe said, handing him a tip.

"Did Geneva tell you room service is available around the clock?" he asked.

"She sure did," Gabe replied. "Oh, I forgot to ask where the bar is located."

"Just past the grand staircase are the open common rooms. There are sitting and dining areas as well as a bar. The last call is two o'clock. There's also a library, billiard room, and a small movie theater on the first floor. Is there anything else I can help you with?" he asked. When we replied we couldn't think of anything, he excused himself and wished us a pleasant evening.

"Just who is Geneva's son?" I asked when we were alone. "Some awesome tennis player?" It was the only sport I knew of that used a court.

"Rodney Louderback is the greatest *basketball* player to ever grace a court, but his charitable deeds and generosity are what makes him a legend in my mind." He pulled me to him for a hard kiss. "Don't be jealous. You're still my Sunshine."

"I'm not jealous." Maybe I was a little bit.

"Uh huh. Why don't you let everyone know we made it while I go down to the bar to get us some mixed drinks. Save me a rocking chair, okay?"

"You got it."

"After the sun goes down, I want to lounge with you in the big tub before I spread blankets on the balcony and make love to you under the stars for the second night in a row."

"Sounds like heaven."

I pulled my phone out of my pocket and noticed I wasn't getting very good cell service. I picked up a second bar once I stepped farther out on the balcony and was able to reach my mom. She was relieved to hear from me and thrilled we loved Tarlington House so much.

"Take a lot of pictures," she told me.

"I will, Mom." She promised to let everyone know we arrived so I could kick back and enjoy what little remained of our first day of vacation.

Gabe returned just in time to watch the sun disappear over the tree line. Peace and tranquility washed over me as day turned to night and the stars appeared, twinkling in the sky. I looked over at Gabe to invite him to the tub but saw he was fast asleep. I set my drink down and went inside to retrieve the throw blanket I saw on the back of the sofa. I started to drape it over him, but he snagged my hand and tugged until I sat on his lap. Gabe tucked me beneath his chin while I covered us up with the blanket. For the second night in a row, I fell asleep in my husband's arms beneath the stars.

SIX

Gabe

I DON'T KNOW HOW LONG I STAYED ASLEEP IN THE ROCKING CHAIR with Josh curled in my arms. Hell, I don't even remember Josh climbing on my lap and covering me with a blanket. The last thing I remember was staring up at the stars in the sky. Fuck, I was getting old. It wasn't too long ago my heat-seeking missile disguised as a dick would've woken me up as soon as Josh was within touching range. I wondered if Josh enjoyed a long, leisurely bath without me. Thinking of him lounging all alone made me sad, but lust swiftly took its place and woke up the rest of me that still slumbered. A naked and wet Josh was one of my favorite visuals.

I trailed my fingers up and down his spine like I usually did, relishing the way he practically purred in his sleep while nestling closer to me. I swear he would burrow into my body like a tick if he could, but he was already entrenched so deep in my heart there was nothing and no one who could ever uproot him. As stiff as I was from a long day of driving and the previous night's uncomfortable sleeping position, I wasn't eager to wake him up and break our connection. Instead, I just sat there and let the serenity of the night wash over me until my eyes felt heavy again.

I started to wake Josh so we could get in bed and sleep more comfortably, but whispering sounds on the wind stilled my hand. A soft chorus of voices rose into the night, making every hair on my body stand at attention. It sounded like it was coming from the woods surrounding the house, but there were no visible signs of people walking in the dark. No lanterns or flashlights gave them away, but I felt their presence just the same. The voices grew louder, and I could hear the verses to the song they sang.

Oh, who will come and go with me?
I am bound for the land of Canaan
I'm bound fair Canaan's land to see,
I'm bound for the land of Canaan.
Oh, Canaan, sweet Canaan,
I'm bound for the land of Canaan
Sweet Canaan, 'tis my happy home;
I am bound for the land of Canaan.
I'll join with those who've gone before,
I am bound for the land of Canaan.
Where sin and sorrow are no more,
I am bound for the land of Canaan.

The voices faded until I could no longer hear them. "Fuck me!" I whispered through teeth that threatened to chatter.

"Okay," Josh said groggily. "I'm always up for a good time."

"Sunshine," I said softly. "I'm pretty sure there were ghosts moving through the woods. They were singing a song I heard in church as a child. 'Sweet Canaan.'"

"It was probably a dream," Josh said sleepily. "We should try to sleep in a real bed tonight. What do you say?"

"It wasn't a dream. I thought it might be at first, but I was wide awake."

Josh rose up so he could look at me. "They're not looking to hurt you. They're just lost souls, wandering the earth."

"How can you be so calm?" I asked. I was freaked the fuck out. "What if Tarlington House has ghosts?"

"It won't upset me unless they hold my head under water or try to ride your cock."

"Those are your hard limits?"

"Think about where we are, Gabe. The South is a hotbed of paranormal activity because of the atrocious crimes against humanity committed here. Who knows how many lost souls are wandering around? It doesn't frighten me; it makes me sad."

"You have a way of putting things in perspective and making me see them in a new light. To me, ghosts were always scary things out to get you."

"That's Hollywood, babe," Josh sleepily said as he rose to his feet. "Scary shit sells, but it doesn't make it accurate." Josh extended his hand, and I pretended not to hear all the popping and cracking going on in my body. "I was going to lead you straight to bed, but I can see a detour is needed."

I followed Josh into our bathroom and undressed while he turned on the faucet to let the water heat up. "Let me," I said when he reached for the hem of his T-shirt. Baring his skin never got old, and I knew it never would. Once he was naked, Josh adjusted the water temperature then put the stop in the drain so the tub would fill. I kept my hands on his body the entire time then pulled him to me for a kiss while we waited for the water to rise.

"I love the way you cherish me," Josh whispered against my lips. "I appreciate all the thought you put into this vacation. I adore being just *us* again."

"I do love and cherish you, Sunshine. It feels like these last few years have flown by like a speeding train. At least at this moment with you, life doesn't feel so damn hectic and insane." I reached around to glide my hand over his taut ass. "I want to slow it down and soak up every second I have with you."

Josh reached over and shut off the faucet. "We'll start with a soak in this amazing tub."

"That's borderline cheesy, Sunshine," I said, stepping into the tub. The water temperature was perfect, but Josh always knew just how I liked everything. "We are a snarky family, not a cheesy one."

"I believe I came up with that rule," he reminded me.

"Well, you nearly broke it."

Josh waited for me to get settled before he stepped over the side of the tub and sank down in the water between my parted thighs. "Oh, hello there, Captain."

How could I not be rock hard with his glorious ass pressed against my cock and balls? Thoughts of soaking my body turned into rowdy fucking. "Turn around and straddle me," I whispered in his ear. Josh must've liked the husky timbre in my voice because he shivered deliciously before doing as I requested.

Josh let his head fall back as soon as our hardened cocks pressed against each other. I took advantage of his exposed neck, knowing how sensitive it was and how horny my kisses made him. The urge to fuck grew stronger every second he was in my arms, but why rush? We were on vacation. We didn't have to set alarms to be up early for work nor would our kids wake us at some ungodly hour. I could kiss and savor him in ways I hadn't in a very long time.

I left no part of my husband's body untouched, and he did

the same to mine. I relearned all the types of kisses that made him shake with want and need. Neither of us let up on our sensual attack until we both trembled against each other. As much as I wanted to be inside Josh, I took my time drying his body then mine before we kissed our way to the bedroom. Turning the bedside lamps off wasn't even a consideration because I didn't want to miss a single expression on his face when we joined our bodies.

I loved the way he reached for me, trusting his heart, body, and soul in my hands. No matter how desperate my lust became, I took my time stretching him open with lubed fingers because I only wanted cries of pleasure crossing his parted lips. I pressed my mouth to Josh's, tasting the passionate cries escaping him when I finally slid home and was fully seated. Josh wrapped his arms around my shoulders and hooked his legs around the back of my thighs, making sure every part of him enveloped every part of me. Just like that, my plans to love him slow and tender evaporated.

Josh grunted into my mouth when I picked up the tempo, driving us both closer to the finish line. Damn, this man made me crazy in all the right ways. "Never...get...enough." I punctuated each word by punching my hips forward, tagging his prostate.

Josh gripped my hair and did his slick maneuver to roll me onto my back, taking control. "I always come out on top," he told me with a mischievous grin before he started to move.

I could do nothing but watch and feel as he mastered me like no one else ever could...or would. My husband was masculine poetry in motion, and I let him taunt me until I couldn't take it anymore.

"God, I love when you lose your control," Josh purred when I rolled him onto his back and became a rutting beast until he came apart beneath me. I was too far gone and filled his ass the moment his face screwed up into his blissed-out orgasm face. "I'm too tired to shower this off," Josh said, pointing to the spunk on his stomach after I collapsed beside him on the bed.

"Give me a few seconds to catch my breath, and I'll get you a warm, wet washcloth," I told him.

"You stay here and rest," Josh said, sitting up in the bed. "You did all the driving while I did all the resting. Besides, you've fallen asleep with me weighing you down two nights in a row."

The bed shifted when he got up, and I heard him walking toward the bathroom. I didn't stay awake long enough to hear him turn on the water, but I roused a little when he cleaned me up with a warm, wet washcloth. I was out again before he finished and didn't wake back up when he climbed beneath the sheets and cuddled up to me. I only knew he cuddled into my side because he always did, and it's how I found him the next morning.

I rolled over onto my side so I could hold him tighter against my chest. I expected us to outgrow our need to tangle our limbs together while we slept, but we hadn't. I had almost drifted back to sleep when I heard a bird doing its morning song thing. For a split second, I thought I was back home in my bed until the bird's morning song was drastically different than anything Savage or Sassy would sing or say. And, it sounded close, and I mean in the same room.

I lifted my head and saw a blue jay perched on the back of a dining room chair. It took a second for my tired brain to register I wasn't dreaming, and the bird was staring right at me. "How'd you get in here?" I asked.

"You brought me," Josh said sleepily. "Damn, you are getting old and forgetful."

"I was talking to the bird who's serenading us this morning." That's when I noticed the doors to the balcony were standing wide open. "Josh, didn't I shut the doors last night when we came in from the balcony?"

"Of course," he said. "You double-checked to make sure they were locked."

"They're wide open now, and this bird invited itself inside our room."

Josh lifted his head and looked over at the blue jay. "Huh. There is a bird in our room, and the doors are hanging wide open. Must be a ghost."

"Or someone let themselves in our room while we slept," I countered.

"You would've heard someone enter our room. I'm pretty sure you sleep with one eye open."

"I slept through the balcony doors opening," I pointed out to him.

"Gabe, you act like you're solving the mystery already."

"What did you say?" I asked. The bird must've realized that things were about to heat up in the room because it flew off.

Josh froze. "Um, what did I say?" he asked, trying to sound confused.

"You mentioned solving a mystery, but how did you know there was going to be a mystery? I never told you about it, and Geneva didn't bring it up last night."

"Um, I think it was in the brochure," Josh hemmed. "Yeah, it must've been." He tried to pull out of my embrace, but I kept a tight grip on him.

"Where do you think you're going?" I asked.

"Bathroom."

"Not until I get some answers out of you." I rolled Josh to his back and positioned myself between his legs. I cupped his balls and gave them a firm but gentle squeeze. "How did you know we would be solving a case?"

"It's going to take a lot more than that to get me to confess," Josh said.

Challenge accepted. I kissed a path down his body until I reached his erect penis. I pressed my tongue against the spot beneath the head that drove him crazy. "Tell me."

"No can do, Captain." Josh tucked his hands behind his head like he was relaxed and prepared to take his torture, but I knew he wouldn't be able to hold out much longer. I was just getting started after all.

I worked him with my tongue and lips, only sucking the head of his cock into my mouth, never giving him exactly what he wanted or taking him to the back of my throat. I knew the friction had to be driving him wild. I split my focus between torturing him and trying to figure it out on my own. I could tell Josh was tired of the games and ready to come but didn't want to be the one to cry mercy.

I released his cock and sat up suddenly in the bed when the answer hit me. "You saw the charge on the credit card statement. That's why you were so chill about riding along with me." Damn, I was disappointed he'd figured it out.

"I didn't go looking for it, babe," Josh said softly. "I would've been surprised had the billing statement not arrived in my email this week."

"Were you ever going to tell me you knew?"

"And ruin your surprise?" he asked. "Why would I? You put so much time and effort into this trip. My knowing in advance didn't change how much I appreciate it, but it might've killed some of the joy for you." He smiled broadly and said, "Live Action Role Play. I didn't know you had it in you, Gabe."

His compliment distracted me enough that it took me a few seconds to realize the LARP event wasn't a separate charge, and it wasn't likely it showed up on the credit card statement which meant he went snooping when he saw the charge on the statement. "You little shit," I said before I dug my fingers in to his inner thighs, tickling him until he kicked and squirmed. "You had to google the inn to know about the event later this week."

Josh's tortured laughter echoed around our room. "I couldn't help myself. I had to know why you chose this place out of more obvious destinations."

"What did you decide the answer was?"

"You are the sweetest and most thoughtful man I know. You're going to let me go Brenda Leigh Johnson on these unsuspecting people."

"I was thinking Sherlock Holmes, but Brenda works too," I admitted.

"You'll bite your tongue and let me run the investigation, right?"

"Of course," I answered quickly. "I think you'll make a wonderful detective."

"We're going to kick LARP ass."

"Sunshine, this is just for fun," I cautioned him. "You don't want to piss off people we have to share the inn with."

"Winning is fun, Gabriel. Do you know what else is fun?"

"Blow jobs before breakfast," I suggested.

"It's like you can read my mind. You should be a cop." Josh crooked his finger at me then added, "Blow jobs before breakfast in the sixty-nine position."

SEVEN

Josh

"I'm starving," I said to Gabe as we made our way down the curving staircases. I just barely resisted the urge to slide down the gleaming banister. "Mmmm. I smell crisp bacon."

"How can you tell it's crispy by the smell?" Gabe asked, doubting my skill.

"Crispy bacon means it cooked longer, so it puts out more bacon-y aroma." My voice sounded sure even though I was guessing.

"You're so full of it," Gabe said, shaking his head.

I leaned closer, nudging him with my shoulder. "I'm so full of you." I grinned when Gabe's face turned a light shade of pink. "Perhaps I did exaggerate my abilities, but I'm willing to wager there's crispy bacon on the breakfast buffet."

"You don't like buffets," Gabe pointed out to me. It was true; I couldn't stand the thought of people touching or sneezing on the food before I put it on my plate. The good Lord knew I adored my children, but kids were the grossest things on the planet. They always had their fingers in their noses or their diapers. It was next to impossible to keep them germ- and bacteria-free. Not to mention flies and bugs landing on uncovered dishes. It was enough to make a man shudder.

"I will survey my surroundings and make a decision. I can always order something from the menu and have it cooked fresh for me." I sounded like the diva I was born to be.

"I'm going to risk life and limb and eat from the buffet," Gabe told me dramatically. "Wait until you see the dining room and gathering areas. They are so beautiful, Sunshine. I thought the woodwork and craftsmanship in our house were amazing, but it's nothing compared to what you're about to see."

"Oh my," I said in awe when I saw the back half of the house where the gathering rooms were located. "I didn't expect the space to be so open. I wasn't even sure it would be appealing, but the rooms are together but separated by the placement of the furniture. Look at the crown molding."

"Isn't it stunning? I couldn't believe my eyes when Rodney showed this house to me," Geneva said, joining us. "How was your first night at Tarlington House? Did you sleep well?"

"We were so tired from traveling we fell asleep while star gazing on the balcony," Gabe said.

"There's nothing like fresh air to help a person fall asleep."

"Geneva," Josh said softly. "I have a question for you that might sound strange."

"I doubt it, but go ahead and try your best to shock me." The red lipstick she wore made her broad smile even prettier.

"Gabe was certain he heard people singing in the forest surrounding the property when he woke up sometime in the middle of the night. It felt spiritual and supernatural to him. Has anyone else ever mentioned this to you?"

"I've heard the songs myself," Geneva replied. "What song did you hear, Gabe? 'Wade in the Water' or 'Sweet Canaan'? Slaves used to sing songs while they worked the fields, but they also used those lyrics to communicate about their escape plans. Since Tarlington didn't have slaves, I think it's echoes of the songs they sang as they made their way through the woods to the rivers. I imagine they had to remain very silent for most of their journey, but once they reached Tarlington land, they could sing out from the bottom of their souls."

Gabe paled when Geneva confirmed he'd probably heard ghosts. "I heard 'Sweet Canaan.' I..." Gabe's words trailed off like he was lost in thought or unsure what to say.

"They won't hurt you, honey. Let me tell you, I wasn't too keen on Rodney buying a former plantation home. I assumed our ancestors were bought, sold, worked to death, and abused here in horrific ways, but then I learned about Jeffrey Tarlington and his efforts to right an egregious wrong. Let me tell you boys, every hair on my body stood up the first time I heard those voices echoing through the darkness. The next morning, I started researching the songs and what those lyrics meant, and I realized those weren't songs of sorrow but of hope. I don't know if they made it safely north; I only know they did everything within their power to try. That's a victory in itself. I can't say if we're hearing ghosts of the slaves walking through the trees at night or the forest is releasing the secrets it's kept all these years. I just know I can feel bone-crushing pain over things that happened here in the South at the same time as I feel pride in my people. It also reminds me not to get complacent."

"I'm sorry to interrupt, Miss Geneva," a young Hispanic lady said. "You have a phone call."

"Excuse me, gentlemen. I didn't mean to keep you from your breakfast. I hope you enjoy," Geneva said, smiling warmly.

"I'd love to hear all about Tarlington House's history sometime," I told her. "Our home in Ohio has significant ties to the Underground Railroad system also. Maybe we can compare stories."

"I'm sure we'll be able to find a quiet spot for an afternoon coffee during your stay," Geneva replied with a wink before walking away, her employee trailing behind her chatting happily.

"Let's check out the buffet," Gabe said. I knew his stomach's demands wouldn't be ignored much longer before it led a revolt.

I followed Gabe into the open, airy dining room. Only a few people were eating at the time, and I wasn't sure if it was because we were earlier or later than the rest of the guests. Some people got up early to cram every experience they could into their days while others used vacation to catch up on sleep and took a leisurely approach. I figured Gabe and I fell into the middle of those two types of vacationers. We weren't eager to get up at the ass crack of dawn, but we did want to experience as much as we could in the hours we were awake.

The first thing I noticed about the buffet was the beautiful layout of the antique sterling silver serving dishes with domed lids. The food wasn't left out in the open for bugs to land on. "Not a booger picker in sight," I whispered to Gabe.

"Unless you consider the ones taller than five feet."

Just when I had worked up my courage to give the buffet a try, my husband had to ruin it. "Gabe," I hissed. He linked our fingers and held tight before I could get away without making a scene.

"You know I'm kidding," he teased. "Just take a look to see what they're offering before you go off half-cocked to find a table and menu."

"Stop winding me up," I said, squeezing his fingers between mine.

"Stop making it so damn easy."

Gabe didn't release my hand until we reached the front of the line. He handed me a plate, and his eyes challenged me to take it. I never backed away from a challenge even when I should. My husband lifted the lid off the first dish and whispered, "Crispy bacon just like you said. I owe you a blow job." We made no such bet, but I wasn't about to refuse his talented mouth. Gabe used the tongs to put several pieces of bacon on both of our plates before we moved to the next dish. There were both sausage patties and links, so Gabe added one of each to both plates. I waved him off when he started to add ham from the third serving dish. "The scrambled eggs are cooked to perfection," Gabe said, gesturing to the fluffy eggs that were dry instead of runny looking. He knew how much I hated wet-looking eggs. The next dish had Southern fried potatoes which included finely diced peppers and onions.

"Don't be stingy," I told him when he added a piddly amount of potatoes. "Worried my ass will get big or something? Afraid I'll bend the pole in my studio?"

"I'm just trying to pace ourselves since there are several more dishes left to explore, and I know how *you* watch what you eat because *you're* worried about those things, not *me*."

"Everybody knows vacation calories don't count, Gabriel," I said haughtily. "More potatoes, please." Gabe pressed a kiss to my temple as he scooped more potatoes onto my plate.

I did pass on the biscuits and gravy even though it looked delicious and smelled better than any I'd ever tried before. *Maybe I'll try a bite of Gabe's.* I chose a large Belgian waffle with a strawberry and banana compote instead of the gravy and biscuits.

"Damn, that looks amazing," Gabe said wistfully. He looked down at his plate and noticed there wasn't any more room to add a waffle, nor was there room for anything else we might find under the remaining lids.

"You can have half of my waffle if you give me a few bites of your biscuits and gravy."

"Deal," Gabe said. "I see some bowls set out by the serving dishes down at the end. I bet you one of them is grits, and not the fake kind you Ohio people make."

"Fake grits?" I asked, following him down the line. "I bet there's real oatmeal under one of those domes. Look at all the toppings they have set up. Brown sugar, cinnamon, raisins. I need to have some oatmeal."

"You people make those instant grits you buy at the store and toss some butter in there and call it a dish. It's just nasty." Gabe sniffed the air like he was following his nose. "Beneath this lid lies real grits made with cornmeal and love." I smiled ridiculously as he whipped the lid off dramatically to reveal his beloved, nasty-ass grits. "You've never had real grits before, Sunshine. This will change your world."

"You'll be wearing those grits if you so much as attempt to spoon them in my mouth. I cannot stand the texture. It's like swallowing buttery sand."

"Sunshine, you're not going to try them?" Gabe asked in a hurt tone.

"Like the way you've refused to try different types of mushrooms?" I countered.

"I cannot stand the texture," Gabe said, repeating my words. I could tell he was fighting off a hard shudder. "Okay, so I understand your aversion to grits. There'll be more for me then," he said, spooning them into a bowl while I helped myself to a small serving of oatmeal.

"If we finish this massive amount of food, then we can explore what's beneath the rest of the lids we didn't open," I told Gabe as we sat down at an empty table.

"Good morning," a tall, lanky guy said as he approached the

table. "I'm Ralph, and I'll be your server this morning. Can I get you something to drink? Coffee? Orange juice?"

Ralph? The kid looked like he was only nineteen years old. He must've been named after a grandfather. "Two coffees," I told him.

"I'll be right back," he replied cheerfully.

Ralph returned a few minutes later with a carafe of coffee, two cups, and a variety of creamers and sugars. "Let me know if you need anything else."

Our mouths were full of food, so we just offered a friendly wave in response. Midway through our meal, a smiling gray-haired lady with a clipboard stopped by our table. "I know you're eating, so I won't take up much of your time. I just wanted to introduce myself quickly. I'm Juliette, and I'm the activities director here. I'm in charge of arranging all the excursions you see in the brochure. My direct line is listed in the contact information, or you can stop by my office. It's on the left side of the registration desk. I hope you'll enjoy your stay."

"Is that like Julie the cruise director?" I asked when we were alone.

"Who?" Gabe asked.

"*Love Boat*," I replied.

"I've never seen the show," Gabe told me with a shrug before he cut himself a chunk of my waffle. "I was surprised to see how many excursions they offered. Horseback riding and a picnic, canoeing and a picnic, jet skis and tubing... I think we're going to have an amazing trip."

"I know we are," I replied.

After breakfast, we exited out of the patio doors between the two gathering areas. There was a large deck offering a gorgeous view of the back lawn which was massive. The entire space was enclosed by a low stone wall covered in flowering vines. There were several outdoor sitting areas beneath canopies to offer shade from the hot sun. Through it all was a paver stone path leading to a wrought iron gate. Beyond the gate, you could see the walking path disappear into the trees.

"Let's see where the path leads," I told Gabe. "I assume it will take us toward the stables where they keep the horses or the river where all the water activities take place."

"I do need to work off some of this food," Gabe replied.

"It would be a beautiful place to read a book," I said to Gabe, gesturing at a comfortable-looking hammock anchored to two large oak trees. "Or nap."

"The online pictures for this place didn't do it justice," Gabe said. "It's amazing."

I wanted to hear the singing Gabe had heard earlier that morning, but the only singing I heard when we strolled hand in hand through the forest was from birds. The path was longer than I expected, but it opened into another flat area with a horse stable and other buildings that appeared to be residential on the left and another winding path through more trees on the right.

"Which do you want to look at first?" I asked Gabe.

"Let's continue on the path. It should lead us to the river. We'll check out the four-legged beasts on our trip back."

We continued down the path, chatting happily or quietly enjoying the solitude until we came to a clearing leading down to a dock where the tied-off jet skis and small boats bounced with the waves as water came to shore. There was a decent-sized wooden structure I figured housed the canoes and life jackets for the water activities. As interesting as I found it to be, my eyes and heart were set on seeing a small lighthouse that was built where the land jutted out like a peninsula. The land appeared to drop off, and I figured there would be a beach below it.

"Gabe, do you remember our fun little competitions on our honeymoon?"

"Do you mean how we tried to outdo each other by planning the perfect excursions?"

"Yep. Care to make a wager right now on who plans the best outing on this vacation?" I asked. I deliberately avoided looking at the lighthouse for too long so he wouldn't guess what my mind was busy creating.

"Challenge accepted," Gabe said smugly. "Let's head back so we can individually chat with Juliette. I'll let you go first while I call Mom and check on the babies."

"No phoning a friend for assistance," I told him.

"I don't need anyone's help," Gabe bragged. "I've got your number."

Yes, he did, but I was still going to blow him away with my surprise.

EIGHT

Gabe

"I NEED THIS TO BE THE MOST ROMANTIC EXCURSION HE'S EVER been on," I told Juliette. "We have young twins at home, and it might be quite some time before we're able to go on vacation again."

"Interesting," she replied, lips tilting up at the corners.

"You probably don't have many couples come in here soliciting your help to out-romance their significant other, do you?"

"No," she agreed with a slight tilt of her head. "I like it though. Josh has made arrangements for tomorrow, so I assume you want to *challenge…I mean romance him on the following day."*

"*That's my goal. Knowing his plans, what might you suggest?*" I listened raptly while she went through some options. "*I want him to weep, Juliette.*" Her eyes widened. "*Happy tears.*" By the time I left her office with an itinerary in hand, I just knew there was no way Josh could top me this time around.

"Wake up, sleepyhead," Josh whispered in my ear the morning of his big adventure.

"Why? We're on vacation," I grumbled.

"We are, and there's no time to waste."

I cracked open one eye to look around the dark room. "It's not even dawn yet."

"That's the point. We need to get up and get an early start. I started the shower for you, and I made you a cup of coffee. The selection of coffees for the Keurig in our room is pretty impressive." *Fuck me!* It sounded like he'd had several cups already. I couldn't say I had any real complaints about my husband. Sure, we all did things that annoyed our spouses, but his cheerfulness first thing in the morning was tipping the scale in favor of complaint instead of a mild annoyance.

I burrowed deeper under the covers, pulling them up to my ears. "Whatever it is you had planned can wait until a decent hour."

"Gabe, I've been up for at least thirty minutes doing yoga on the balcony so I could be good and limber for what I had planned for you."

Yoga. Limber. Those two words jumpstarted my brain and dick to life. Watching Josh do yoga was better than watching porn. I threw back the covers and sat up. "Why didn't you wake me up for that?"

"Because it leads to sex, and I need to hold off on that for just a while."

You know the sound an engine makes as it winds down when you shut it off? Yeah, that was my cock. No sex?

"I didn't say we weren't having sex," Josh said, jerking back the covers. Had I said it out loud? "We're having sex in a very special place as part of my special day. You can come back afterward and take a nap." I don't know at what age taking a nap went from something I loathed to something I loved, but it almost ranked as high as sex on some occasions.

"Okay," I grumbled as I rose from the bed and started zombie-shuffling toward the bedroom. "This better rock my world."

"Don't I always?" Josh asked.

"Yes, but it doesn't mean I'm not questioning the date I planned for you. I now think I was too kind." Josh's happy laughter followed me into the bathroom and made me smile when I wasn't in the mood.

"Don't jerk off either," Josh said as I began lathering my body.

"Worried I won't be able to get it up again so soon?"

Josh snorted. "I just don't want to be late, so no lingering on your cock and balls."

The sky was still fairly dark by the time I joined Josh on the balcony. "Washed, dried, and dressed. Now what?"

"Now we leave."

"Leave? Where are we going?"

"Do you trust me?"

"Of course, I trust you," I replied.

"Then just follow me."

I followed him down the main staircase through the common rooms to the French doors leading to the gorgeous deck on the back of the inn. Through the wall of eastward-facing windows, I could see the sky lightening up a bit as the sun was thinking about making its glorious appearance. Josh opened the doors and stepped onto the deck.

"Good morning," Juliette cheerfully said, startling me. She was the last person I expected to be awake at such an ungodly hour, although, I realized the inn staff would be up and at it early to get everything prepared for the day. Somehow, I doubted meeting guests on the deck before dawn was part of her normal duties. "This should be everything you requested, Josh." Juliette handed him a picnic basket, a flannel blanket, and two flashlights. *Flashlights? Where the hell were we going?*

"Thank you so much, Juliette." Josh then looked over the trees to the horizon. "We better get a move on before we miss it." Josh handed me a flashlight then clicked his on.

"Miss what?" I asked, obediently following him. "Thank you, Juliette," I tossed over my shoulder when I remembered my manners.

"My pleasure, gentlemen."

"Sunshine, are you expecting me to walk through the haunted forest in the dark?"

"It's enchanted, not haunted. No one is going to hurt you. There will only be pleasure during this excursion. Toe-curling pleasure." I admittedly picked up the pace a little. Josh inhaled dramatically and released his breath slowly when we entered the darkened woods. "Smell it?"

I took a deep breath, picking up the scents of pine, grass, and dirt. I would never have taken Josh as a nature boy, but he seemed damned eager to trek through the woods that morning. "Earth?" I asked.

"Renewal. Growth. Promise."

"Babe, I'm finding this new side of you very interesting, but I hope there's something more exciting than twigs and berries in your picnic basket."

"Man can't live on twigs and berries alone," Josh replied.

My senses were on high alert when we walked through the woods. Not only was it dark, the feeling of being observed added to the creepiness factor. I couldn't say if it was human or ethereal, but the hair was standing up all over my body, telling me we weren't alone. I stepped closer to Josh without trying to make it obvious I was ready to spring into action. I was probably being ridiculous, but the singing in the woods and the open balcony door after I specifically remember closing and locking it left me feeling uneasy.

We came to the first clearing where the barns and additional living quarters were located, and I noticed there wasn't a single light on in any of the structures. I never asked if those buildings were where the staff lived, I'd just assumed. They were either all at work or they were still sleeping like I wished I was. Not even the horses were stirring in the barns. I thought farmers were up before dawn feeding their pets. Tarlington House was still an active farm with hundreds of acres of farmland surrounding it. Where were the farmhands?

"Stop grumbling," Josh said, making a turn toward the second trail in the woods leading to the river.

"I didn't say anything," I replied.

"I saw you eyeing the living quarters and barn. I bet you were wondering why you were up before them." *Did he always need to be right?* "I promise this will be the only morning I wake you before dawn."

"Okay," I grumbled.

The sky had lightened up some more by the time we made it to the second clearing leading to the inlet where Steamboat Creek met North Edisto River, but the sun was only flirting with the horizon.

"Wow," I said out loud. "This will be an incredible place to watch the sunrise."

"You haven't seen anything yet." Josh nodded his head toward the lighthouse where soft glowing lights flickered in the windows. "Come on," he told me. "I want to make sure everything is set up perfectly for your surprise."

I could've told him that standing in the clearing was perfect enough, but I could tell how important this was to him. Not only because of the competition we had going on between us either. He was proud of his plan, and I wouldn't spoil it. Plus, he did mention something about sex, and I had a pretty good idea of exactly what he planned.

The lighthouse was locked, but Josh retrieved the key out of the picnic basket to let us inside. The flickering lights in the windows were electric LED candles and a lovely touch. I wondered if someone came in later to turn them off or if they had sensors triggered by the amount of light to turn them on and off. The interior of the lighthouse maintained the original woodwork just like Tarlington House. This wasn't some ramshackle, crumbling building. It smelled of history and Murphy's Oil Soap. Someone took great care in its upkeep.

I saw the winding metal staircase in the center of the room and followed it up until it disappeared into an opening in the floor above us. I knew it was our destination and eagerly followed Josh up those hundreds of steps to reach the lookout point.

"Oh my God!" I said, looking over the river. "Sunshine, this is…" My words trailed off.

"We haven't seen anything yet. Keep your eye on the horizon while I unpack the picnic basket."

I sat in one of the Adirondack chairs facing the horizon over the river while Josh bustled around behind me making a nest. "Why don't you leave it alone for now and come watch the sunrise with me? I doubt you intended for me to witness it by my lonesome."

"Just let me pour us a cup of coffee."

"It can wait," I told him. "I want you in my arms, preferably naked."

Josh came to stand in front of me and immediately began undressing. "Getting naked was part of the plan." He reached into his pocket and pulled out a packet of lube then tossed it to me so he could finish pushing his pants down his legs. Behind him, the horizon was beginning to turn orange, yellow, and pink. As beautiful as the sunrise promised to be, there would never be anything that made my heart pound and blood race with excitement more than looking at my husband. *My husband.*

I expected Josh to climb on my lap, but he crooked his finger for me to follow him onto the wraparound gallery. "Lose your clothes too."

Strutting around nude wasn't high on my list, but I saw the concrete wall surrounding the gallery was high enough to protect us from the prying eyes of anyone who happened to be up at the ridiculously early hour. When I stepped onto the gallery, the top of the sun was just emerging from her slumber, but it wasn't what captured my attention. Josh leaned his upper body on top of the wall, popping his delicious ass out on display.

He felt my stare and looked over his shoulder, pulling my eyes up to meet his. "You're going to miss the sunrise staring at my ass."

"I'm not going to miss a thing," I said, stepping behind him and cupping his ass with both hands. "I'm skilled enough to make love to you while watching the sun come up."

Josh moaned and pushed back into my touch when I began kneading his ass. "I was hoping you would say that."

"Just keep your eyes on the horizon, Sunshine."

I dropped to my knees and rimmed his puckered hole until I was able to work my tongue inside him then I reached for the packet of lube I dropped by his feet. "Y-y-ou're going to miss it."

I squirted lube on my fingers then stood up to take my place behind him. "I'm exactly where I want to be." He gasped and moaned when I slid my first slick digit inside to tease him. "You're my personal sunrise and sunset, Josh. Nothing will ever compare to you, to this." I slid a second finger inside him, working them in and out to stretch him as the sun inched a little higher.

"Damn, how do you always know the right thing to say?" he asked breathily.

I didn't always say the right things, but it was easy for him to forget in the heat of passion. "I speak from the heart."

I removed my fingers and lined my dick up to his greedy hole. "And I love making love to you more than breathing." I slowly eased inside him until my pelvis was flush against his pert ass. "But this you already know." Josh turned his head, his mouth seeking mine. I couldn't deny him anything he wanted, so I kept our kiss shorter than I preferred. "Eyes on the sunrise." Then I began to move in deep, slow strokes. I silently vowed our lovemaking would last as long as it took for the sun to fully rise which meant I had to stop a few times to touch and tease him in other ways. Josh thought I was edging him, but I just wanted to give us both a sunrise we'd never forget. After all, we weren't guaranteed another together. What if this was the only one we had left? If I couldn't come, he couldn't either.

"I need to come," Josh pleaded.

"Almost," I said when just the tiniest sliver of the sun hadn't risen above the horizon. "A few more minutes." When the sun was fully visible, I linked my fingers with Josh's on the concrete wall and quickened my strokes just the way we both liked it. "Come with me, Sunshine." And he did.

Afterward, I wanted to lean against him, but I didn't want my weight to crush him against the rough concrete. Instead, I slowly pulled out and tugged him back to lean against me.

"This is going to be hard to beat," Josh said proudly. "Romantic, sexy, and beautiful. Oh, and you haven't seen what's inside the basket yet."

I had forgotten all about the food. Josh turned in my arms, rose up on his tiptoes, and kissed me. "We'll see if you feel so confident when you see what I have planned for you tomorrow."

"I'm sure it will be nice."

"*Nice?*"

"Don't get your tighty-whities in a twist," Josh said, pulling out of my arms and heading back inside the lighthouse.

"I'm not wearing any," I reminded him.

"It's a figure of speech, Gabriel. You don't even own a pair of tighty-whities which is something I think we need to correct. I also think you need to get them wet accidentally."

"How do you suppose I get them wet? Do you want me to run through our yard in the rain?" I wasn't aware Josh found old-fashioned white briefs to be attractive. Wait. He didn't say anything about them being the kind of underwear men in their eighties wore.

"Babe, it kind of kills the fantasy a bit if I have to spell it out for you. It's so much more fun for me to see what you come up with on your own." Josh put his underwear back on then spread out the blanket on the wood floor before placing the basket in the center and plopping down beside it.

I followed his lead even though I didn't know why we couldn't be naked just a little longer.

"Do we want to return the blanket with dried cum on it?"

As always, he made an excellent point. "What surprises do you have in there?" Josh opened the basket, and the obvious smells of apples, cinnamon, and sugar wafted out. "I smell apple pie." Josh pulled out a package of wet wipes so we could clean off our hands before eating.

"You smell apple pie muffins," he corrected. "I hope you won't be disappointed." Josh split a muffin in two and spread butter on only one half, handing the butter-free half to me. My husband swore butter enhanced muffins, but we agreed to disagree.

"They're still warm," I said before I took a bite. "Mmmm. Good." Josh grinned when I talked with food in my mouth because it was the ultimate compliment to the chef or baker. When my pleasure for the bite of food overrode decades of good upbringing, you know I'm onto something truly special.

"I have many other things planned for us later today, but you'll be happiest about Juliette's promise to share this recipe with me. You'll be transported back to this moment every time I make these muffins for you at home."

Josh's hair was sticking up everywhere, and his skin was still damp with sweat from our lovemaking. He'd never looked more beautiful to me, and I would happily relive this moment for the rest of my life.

NINE

Josh

"Why are you FaceTiming me when you're on vacation with your husband?" Mere asked me.

"I'm not FaceTiming you; I'm FaceTiming Tori," I replied. "I swear she's changed so much already."

"You've only been gone for a few days, Jazz."

"A lot can happen in a few days. She looks so beautiful in the little floral dress and baby pink cardigan we bought her. Kiss her for me."

"I will."

"Do it now." I inhaled a deep breath like I could smell her lavender lotion and shampoo. "I want to watch."

"You need help," Mere said.

"This is news?" Gabe asked Mere when he joined me on the couch in our suite. He looked over at me and said, "I was concerned about what you were instructing someone to do so you could watch."

"Yeah, because you've caught me interacting with live webcam shows so many times."

"I thought maybe you got bored with me since my surprise outing was canceled due to the rain and went looking for some entertainment."

I saw in his eyes how disappointed he was that his plans were ruined, but I wasn't. Discreetly making love with Gabe on our private balcony while the rain poured from the sky was the sexiest thing I'd ever done. The balcony had a roof on it, but the rain came in at the perfect angle to drench us good. "Best. Date. Ever."

"Um, guys," Mere said then giggled. "How about you call back after you've worked each other out of your system."

"That will never happen," Gabe and I said at the same time.

"All the same, Queen V is waking up and searching out her next meal. I know you're both enlightened gentlemen and all, but breastfeeding on FaceTime isn't my idea of a fun time."

"Fine, but I want to be sure you're giving Tori the kisses I've sent her each day. I'll wait."

Mere giggled and placed a lingering kiss on Tori's forehead. "That kiss is from your uncles, Josh and Gabe. They love you so much."

"Bye, Mere and Tori. We'll chat later."

Mere blew me an air kiss before she disconnected. I leaned into Gabe, and he put his arm around me. "We've video chatted with our kids and Mere. Chaz is up to his armpits in edits, so I will only receive short replies from him until he meets his deadline."

"Are you bored?" Gabe asked me.

"Hell no, Captain Sexy Pants. I'm just one of those persons who likes to keep busy. The rain has prohibited us from doing much outside, so I'm using the quiet time to catch up with the people we love back home. Don't pretend you haven't checked in with Adrian to see if everything was running smoothly."

"Of course," Gabe admitted. "Adrian has everything under control though."

"You won."

"It's nice to know I'm better than you at something, even if it's rummy."

"Gabe, I wasn't talking about the card game. I meant the little competition between us. You won."

"Josh," Gabe said tenderly. "You don't need to make me feel better about my failed plans. You gave me the most beautiful sunrise ever witnessed by man. There's no comparison between it and the picnic lunch we had in our suite."

"The lunch was filled with my favorite foods. I sat across from you on a blanket in this lovely home. Then we played card games which ended with us making love on our balcony with the rain pouring down on our naked skin. Do you think I'll ever forget the sounds you made when you came or the way it felt to fill your ass in such a primal, natural way? You didn't let the rain ruin our day; you used it to your advantage. It was perfection."

"It was truly special," Gabe admitted. "Juliette assured me I'd have plenty of time to reschedule our date though."

"It's not necessary."

"You say that now because you don't know what I had planned."

"True," I said with a shrug, "but you've already won, and I doubt you can outdo the rainy lovemaking."

"I can give it my best shot."

Who was I to discourage my husband from wowing me? "If

you insist," I replied in a resigned voice. Gabe smirked because he knew I was already planning to outdo him. It was my nature, so why fight it? "I'm challenging you to some board games next. I think Clue would be a great idea since we will have a murder mystery to solve in a few days."

"You've had plenty of practice on your iPad, and I've had real-life experience to give me a leg up."

"Will you at least show me the costumes?"

"Nope."

"Will you give me a hint?"

"No."

"Fine," I said. Just then, I heard a car pulling up in front of the inn. "Oh, I wonder if our competition is starting to arrive."

"Could be," Gabe agreed. "We're here as part of an extended vacation, so it only seems reasonable others would do the same."

"And doing a bit of recon while they're at it."

"Want to check out our competition, Sunshine?"

"Does your dick wake up happy to see me?" I answered his rhetorical question with one of my own. I'd sent our mothers undercover to salons that opened in neighboring communities. Hell yes, I wanted to see who I was up against.

Gabe and I went onto the balcony. The rain was barely a drizzle by this time, so we could observe the new arrivals without it looking too obvious. "Wow," Gabe said in awe when he spied the shiny, black vehicle pulling to a stop in front of the inn. "A person doesn't see a Rolls-Royce every day."

"And?" I asked. I'd heard of the car company but didn't understand the significance of Gabe's implications.

Before Gabe could answer, José jogged down the steps holding a large umbrella with the inn's logo on it. He opened the passenger door and extended his hand to the woman sitting inside. The lady placed a gloved hand, yes, gloved, in his and graciously swung her legs around and exited the car. I couldn't see her face because of the large hat she wore.

"It's Queen Elizabeth," I said in an exaggerated whisper.

The driver, also wearing a dapper hat, exited the car and jogged around the front to join José and, I assumed, his wife. I couldn't hear what they said, but the voices and body language spoke of their familiarity with the valet.

"Repeat guests," Gabe said.

José moved in to place a kiss on the woman's cheek. "They're awfully chummy with the staff," I added. "It won't stop us from taking Thurston and Lovey Howell down."

Gabe snorted. "I'm almost more excited about the snarky code names you'll give our competitors than I am the actual murder mystery we need to solve."

"What do you think they'll call us? The Fabulous Two?"

Gabe threw his head back and laughed at my suggestion, pulling the attention of the newly arrived guests and José upward. Thurston gave us a friendly nod while Lovey narrowed her eyes.

"I think you stole her suite," I whispered to Gabe.

"Don't care," he replied. "Lord only knows when we'll get another vacation, so she can stew about it all she wants. Distract her from solving the crime." He winked playfully and pulled me back inside our suite.

"Do you think other guests will arrive today too? The actual event doesn't start until Friday night."

"I think it's a great possibility. Do we stay up here and scope out our competition, or do we act less obvious and do it from the common rooms downstairs?"

"Downstairs," I replied eagerly. I wanted to see these people in action.

The Howells were still checking in after we descended the staircase. I only glanced in their direction, but it was enough to tell me a lot. I might not have recognized their sleek-ass ride, but I recognized Louis Vuitton luggage and handbags when I saw them. I also noticed the bright red sole of her Christian Louboutin stilettos.

"Her pair of shoes probably cost as much as a mortgage payment," I whispered to Gabe as we headed into the seating area in the great room. "Oh, the gas fireplace is a nice touch on a rainy day," I said. "I brought my Kindle to read on."

"I have the latest Clancy paperback."

We each grabbed a cup of coffee and settled in where we could observe the front desk without being too obvious. I observed Juliette and Geneva greeting the Howells with hugs also.

"I find them interesting," Gabe said while continuing to look at his paperback book. "I don't associate people who can afford a car costing a quarter of a million dollars with people who hug the staff at the inn."

"Not all wealthy people are stuck-up assholes." I shifted my attention back to the Kindle, but even Chaz's skill couldn't keep my attention for long.

"Of course not, Sunshine. There's a big difference between showing courtesy to the staff at the inn and hugging them like they're long-lost cousins."

"True." He made a valid point. His detective skills were going to come in handy when the real games began.

"I've been around some of the world's wealthiest people in Miami, and I have to say they were a lot more subtle about displaying their wealth."

"What do you think it means?" I asked.

"New money."

"Like they've won the lottery?" I asked.

"Yes, or a lawsuit of some sort."

"Interesting," I replied. My phone vibrated in my pocket, and I saw it was a text from Chaz when I retrieved it.

I'm not so sure about this book, Josh.

I set my Kindle down and quickly typed a response. *Why? I fucking love it.*

Really? Not too...taboo?

Yes, really. If I'm honest, this is your best writing. Their longing and passion for each other is a palpable thing.

Chaz came back quickly... *I don't know. I've never felt this uncertain.*

I felt his confusion coming through the message and wished I could give him a reassuring hug. *Sometimes you have to push outside your comfort zone. What's the worst that can happen?*

People could think I'm a pervert and stop reading my books.

I scowled down at my phone for a minute while I thought of the right words to say.

"Everything okay?" Gabe asked.

"Yeah, Chaz is just feeling unsure about his new book. Keep an eye on the competition."

"I'm on it, Sunshine."

I glanced up from my phone when I felt someone staring at me. Lovey wore an inscrutable expression as she focused her attention on me while Thurston conversed with the lady behind the registration counter. In return, I raised a brow. A slow smile spread across her face, but it looked more like the way Angelina smiled when she played Maleficent than a friendly gesture.

"Making an impression, I see," Gabe said.

"Did you see that? Lovey is throwing down." I answered her sly smile with one of my own, signaling I accepted her challenge.

My phone vibrated again with another text message. *Hello? Are you still there or did you ditch me for vacation sex? I can't blame you.*

Sorry. The first couple in our murder mystery competition just showed up. I'm calling them Thurston and Lovey.

Super rich?

I narrowed my eyes as I watched them walk toward us. The suave grace I expected from the super rich was missing. Were they wealthy people or playing dress up? Were the car and clothes all a part of their role playing?

So it seems, I answered Chaz. *Listen, I won't tell you how to do your job or tell you to publish a book that makes you feel uncomfortable.*

But…

I think you should have a heart-to-heart talk with your fans on your SM sites. Give them enough information to form an opinion without spoiling the book. There's also the summation thingy on the back of the book. What's it called?

Chaz sent a laughing emoji. *It's called the blurb. Most of us call it the "fucking blurb."*

Fine, I said. *Give it to them straight in the "fucking blurb," and they can choose to read it or not. It's not like you're holding a gun to anyone's head.*

True. Chaz sent a heart emoji followed by, *You've made me feel so much better. So, you like it?*

Like? I freaking love it.

We spend the next twenty minutes or so texting back and forth about the book. Chaz accidentally gave away a spoiler when he asked a question about a part I hadn't read yet. Instead of getting mad, it made me want to read more which was what I told him before I shoved my phone back in my pocket.

"What'd I miss?" I asked Gabe.

"Thurston tried to discreetly grab Lovey's ass while they walked up the steps."

"What did she do?"

"She recoiled and practically pushed him down the stairs."

"Wow," I said. "This keeps getting better and better. It seems like an overreaction."

"I'm interested to see how they act during dinner. I get some people aren't into public displays of affection, but knocking the guy down the steps seems extreme."

Juliette made her way over to our table. She wore her usual happy-to-help smile and carried her ever-present clipboard. "How was your picnic lunch? Was it to your satisfaction?"

"It exceeded my expectations," Gabe told her. "My husband is probably the best cook I've ever known, and he was very impressed with the chicken salad on croissants."

"The chef didn't skimp on seasoning just because it was a sandwich. I saw he or she added fresh rosemary, and I have mad respect for those kinds of special touches," I told Juliette. "Also, I liked how the nuts and fruit were finely and uniformly chopped. My highest compliments to the chef because this is a person who knows a properly made sandwich is an art form."

Juliette threw back her head and laughed. "I'll be sure to let Pierre know how much you loved the chicken salad. Maybe he should consider adding it to the menu."

Her remark confirmed how committed Gabe was to provide the perfect picnic lunch for us. "He definitely should. Did he make those barbecue potato chips himself? They were delicious."

"Everything in the basket was made by Pierre with love including the mayonnaise used in the dressing. Geneva stole him away from a four-star restaurant a few years ago. It was one of the best decisions she's ever made."

"Get out of here," I said excitedly. "In theory, I know only a few ingredients go into mayonnaise, but I've never attempted to make my own." Gabe snorted because he knew it would change as soon as we got home. A speculative gleam was also present.

"What are you up to?" I asked him.

"You'll find out," Gabe replied before turning his attention back to Juliette. "Can we have a private chat."

I went back to reading, but my focus was split between the words, watching for the Howells, and Gabe's return. I was dying to know what he was planning and knew it was good when he returned looking like the smuggest man on earth.

"Don't even bother asking," he told me when I opened my mouth. "Let's focus on how we're going to strike up a conversation with Thurston and Lovey."

We talked over some strategies for a bit but realized it wasn't necessary when the couple came down to the gathering area and approached us after they got drinks at the bar. I respected their bold move, but I still planned on kicking their ass when I solved the mystery before them.

TEN

Gabe

"Hello," the man said in a genteel Southern drawl. "My name is George Howard, and this is my wife, Georgia." I knew Josh would have a blast with how cutesy their names were, but I suspected they were using names as fake as their relationship appeared to be. There was zero familiarity or closeness between them. I knew marriages were more like business arrangements in the wealthiest classes in America, but these people left me feeling cold enough to put on a jacket.

Josh and I rose to our feet and politely shook their hands. I noticed George's handshake was firm and his fingers were heavily callused, indicating he most likely worked with his hands. I was eager to find out what he said he did for a living. His *wife's* handshake was soft and very brief like she was afraid to sully her hands.

"I'm Gabriel, and this is my husband, Josh."

"Where are you from?" George asked. "I don't detect an accent." Southerners were known for speaking slow, but George's speech cadence seemed contrived.

"We're from Ohio," Josh replied.

"Ah, Yankees then." The good-natured smile George aimed at us to soften the context of his words was as fake as the rest of him.

"Darling," Georgia purred, but it sounded more like dahling. "The war has been over for a very long time. I think we can let it go."

"If it helps, Gabe is originally from Florida, and we live in Southern Ohio," Josh offered then giggled. My husband never *giggled*. What was he up to? I also noticed his movements and gestures were more exaggerated than usual. I realized he was getting into a role just like these two posers were. I couldn't see where he was taking this.

"That works for me. Let's all sit down and get to know one another," George suggested. "How long are you fellas staying?" Yep, he was feeling us out to see if we were part of the murder mystery weekend.

"Until Sunday," Josh said then clapped his hands excitedly. "How about you?"

"The same," Georgia replied coolly. "Is this your first stay at Tarlington House?"

"It is our first trip, but it won't be our last," I replied.

George leaned forward and lowered his voice. "So, you've heard about the silly little murder mystery they host?"

Josh mimicked George's actions, and it was all I could do not to laugh. "We have heard. It sounds like a lot of fun."

"Have you attended anything like this before?" Georgia asked while staring into the drink she lazily stirred. I liked how they were casually sizing us up the same way we were doing with them.

"Oh no!" Josh replied dramatically. "This is the first time we attempted anything so wild."

Georgia looked up from her drink and studied Josh through slightly narrowed eyes. He might've been overplaying his hand just a bit. "What do you gentlemen do for a living?"

"Gabe is a professor, and I'm a stay-at-home dad." *Professor?* I could see that he wouldn't want our competitors to know I solved crimes for a living, but someone who was put in charge of educating others? *Stay-at-home dad?* That was the exact opposite of who he was. Josh was a dedicated father who would rearrange his schedule at a moment's notice for our babies, but he needed work to feel balanced.

"Interesting," George said with a raised brow. "What did you do before you had children?"

I held my breath while waiting to see what Josh came up with. My husband was proud of the business he built and didn't care if people saw him as a cliché. He would remind people that he wasn't just a hair stylist, he was the motherfucking owner of a very successful salon. He was never embarrassed about his job, so I was eager to see how he would play this one.

"I was a dancer," Josh replied with a smile. "Well, I still am when I find the time in my busy schedule."

"Dancer, huh? Ballet?" George asked before taking a sip of his drink.

"Pole," Josh corrected cheekily.

George started to choke and spat his drink back in his glass, but he overshot, and some of it splashed on his pressed trousers.

"Oh, for fuck's sake," Georgia snapped, letting her true self show. "What's the matter with you?" She shook her head, aimed a brittle smile at us then stood up. "We need to return to our room to freshen up. Please accept our apology for abruptly ending this lovely chat." I thought she recovered her composure well.

"It's no problem," I said. "I'm sure we'll have ample opportunities to resume our conversation."

"Indeed," George said, rising to his feet. "Until we meet again." He saluted us with his glass.

We didn't say anything until they disappeared up the steps and were out of sight. I turned to my husband and said, "Professor?"

"It was the first thing that came to mind," he replied with a shrug. "I mean, you did teach me how to love."

"That's so fucking sweet," I said. "We need to go up to our room."

Josh waggled his brows. "You want to teach me a new trick?"

"Always, but I was thinking more like we need to strategize. Get our stories straight."

"Is this a clothing-optional meeting?"

"Does my dick wake up happy to see you?" I countered.

When we returned to the dining room for dinner, we saw that George and Georgia were already there and were joined by another couple. Where I placed the Howards to be in their mid-fifties to early sixties, the newcomers looked to be in their early thirties. They were both blond-haired and blue-eyed, and their body language told me they hadn't just met the Howards.

George glanced up and suddenly stopped speaking when he saw us. He gestured for Josh and me to join them, so I placed my hand on Josh's lower back and guided him to their table. "Good evening," I said, hoping I sounded professor-ish.

"Good evening," George replied. I had to hand it to him. Georgia's veneer had cracked, but his hadn't. Yet. George looked to his guests and said, "This is the couple I told you about. They're also here to have a little fun."

"Is that so," the young lady said, looking me up and down like I was a snack. "This looks to be a very *fun* weekend."

I moved my hand from Josh's lower back and placed it on his neck when I felt him tense. He hadn't missed her boldness either, but he relaxed beneath the gentle squeeze I gave him. I wasn't going anywhere, and he damn well knew it. "I'm Gabe, and this is my husband, Josh."

"I'm Henry, and this is my sister, Petal," the younger guy said. "Why don't you have a seat and join us. We haven't ordered our meals yet."

"Of course," Josh said, pulling out the chair in front of him. "We'd love to join you."

The waiter rushed over and dropped off menus for Josh and me then took our drink orders. I wanted a clear head to keep score, but I also thought a drink might help me relax a bit. I ordered a Scotch, neat, while Josh ordered some fussy drink I'd never heard of. I knew we'd rib each other over the drink choices as soon as we were alone again. I rarely drank hard liquor because beer was my choice of alcohol. I just thought Scotch sounded professor-y.

"George and Georgia told us a little about you, but I'm dying to hear more," Petal purred. Of course, she only aimed that remark in my direction.

Josh and I decided our best strategy for not slipping up was to keep our story as close to nonfiction as possible. We agreed that our jobs were the only lie we were willing to tell. "Josh and I still consider ourselves newlyweds because we're a few months shy of our two-year anniversary. We have adorable twins, a son and a daughter, and we're making plans to extend our family even more next year."

"Which one of you carries the babies?" Henry asked then laughed like his joke was funny.

"They use surrogates or adopt children," Georgia answered, sounding appalled by the question. She offered me a smile, and it appeared to be the first genuine reaction I got from her. Maybe she wasn't so bad.

"I know," Henry guffawed. "I'm not that ignorant." *That was debatable.* "My apologies, gentlemen. I didn't mean to offend you."

"I assure you we've heard worse," Josh said while casually perusing the menu. Of course, I had my hand on his thigh beneath the table and felt how tense his body was. "Since you've all been here before, what do you recommend from the menu?"

Each of them told us their favorite entrée, side dish, and appetizer which allowed us time to see how they interacted with one another. The more they talked, the more it became obvious they knew each other very well. Georgia reminded Petal that she had loved the herb-encrusted asparagus ever since it was added to the menu, and Henry chose George's answer for him when he couldn't decide between the blackened sea bass and pan-seared, aged prime rib.

"It's always the prime rib," Henry said affectionately.

Josh slid his hand along my thigh, letting me know he was picking up on all the clues as well. If he went much higher, my focus would be diverted south. God, I couldn't get enough of the man sitting beside me.

"Pardon me for saying this, but the four of you seem well-acquainted," Josh said. "Have you all been coming to this murder mystery event for several years, or are you friends?"

"I wouldn't say we're *friends.*" Georgia sounded like the idea was offensive. She offered a chilly smile to Petal who looked upset. "We are acquainted with one another."

"George, our conversation was interrupted before you could share with us what you do for a living," I told him.

"Ah yes," the older man said, sitting taller in his chair. "I'm an investment banker."

He didn't say with what firm which made me doubt him even

more. I've been around that type plenty of types and the words "investment banker" are always followed up by the firm they represent. How else are they going to grow business? "Are you from South Carolina?"

Georgia and Petal both snorted like the idea was ludicrous. They upped their snobbishness to a new level. Perhaps that part wasn't an act. "Hardly, love," Petal said to me. "We're all from Atlanta."

"I've been to Atlanta a few times," Josh said. *He had?* "I've won some competitions there."

"What kind of competitions?" Petal asked, looking at my husband for the first time since we arrived.

"Dance," Josh replied.

"Talent show competitions?" Henry asked.

Josh, the comedian that he was, waited for Henry to take a drink of his wine before answering. "Pole dancing."

Henry didn't choke, but his eyes widened, and he licked his lips while studying the parts of my husband he could see. "You do look flexible and maybe another word that starts with F and ends with b-l-e." Josh dug his nails into my jeans. Why? Had I growled? I was prone to do so when someone looked at my husband the way Henry was.

"Gabe thinks so," Josh said.

"Do you still dance?" Petal asked, tipping her head to the side like she was genuinely curious.

"Only privately," my husband replied, leaning into me so that his head was against my shoulder.

"You can't have time for that with two kids," Henry said. "I'm sure your marriage has gone stale even if you haven't been married long."

"On the contrary," Josh said, looking up at me. "You find time for the things that are important to you. Quality time alone with my guy is at the top of the list. I refuse to believe I have to choose between our children and Gabe. I save energy and time for him."

Henry held up his wine glass as if he was toasting me. "You're a lucky man, Gabe."

"That I am, Henry."

"So, George is an investment banker," Josh said. "What about you, Georgia. Do you work outside the home?"

George snorted, earning a bitter glare from his *wife*. "I am on the board for many charities to raise money for important causes. That keeps me very busy."

"Maybe you can have a chat with Josh on how to juggle things so you have time for your husband?" George suggested.

"Dear, this sort of conversation is beneath our station in life," Georgia reprimanded him.

"*Dear*," George mocked, "I wasn't talking about your dislike of performing blow jobs. I was merely stating that it would be nice if you could find time doing something other than spending my money or finding excuses to get drunk in the middle of the afternoon. But since we're on the topic, perhaps you could make more time to suck my dick instead of your personal trainer's."

Georgia gasped loudly and stood up so fast her chair fell backward. "You son of a bitch," she snarled before leaving the room with her head held high and shoulders squared. I had no idea if any of what we witnessed was true, but the woman was in incredible shape, so I suspected that she at least employed a personal trainer.

"Actually, *George*," Petal said. I bit my lip to keep from smiling when she emphasized his fake name. "Her personal trainer is a woman." Petal stood up and exited the room without saying another word to any of us.

I glanced up at Henry, who watched her walk away. The way he stared at her ass wasn't the way a brother stared at his sister. He must've felt my scrutiny because he snapped his head in my direction. I didn't verbally remark on what I witnessed; I just raised an eyebrow. His reply was a quick shrug and a crooked smile before he chugged the rest of his wine.

"Well, hell," George drawled slowly. "The least she could do is let me watch."

Henry clapped him on the back then laughed. "I'm going to get drunk. Who is with me?"

Josh and I looked at each other and shrugged. It had been a long time since either of us drank enough to be considered more than warm and fuzzy. I thought to myself, *why the hell not?*

Of course, the next morning when I was hugging the toilet bowl, I remembered all the reasons why I didn't get drunk anymore.

"Here, baby," Josh softly said as he pressed a cold washcloth against my forehead. "Do you think you're done vomiting?"

I thought I was, but then again, I'd thought the same thing before the second round of puking. I tried to nod, but it felt like someone drove an ax through my head. "Why aren't you hungover?" Fuck, my voice sounded like I'd just smoked two cartons of cigarettes and gargled with battery acid.

"Because one of us needed to get the skinny on our competition."

"I'm married to an evil genius," I said proudly.

"An evil genius who knows a few tricks to make your hangover go away fast so we can continue with the second phase of my plan."

"Second phase?" I asked.

"It involves fake fights and fake makeup sex. Well, the sex will be real but not the purpose behind it."

"I'm in."

ELEVEN

Josh

"I don't remember a whole lot about last night," Gabe said sluggishly. "I didn't give too much away, did I?"

"I protected your virtue, Captain Morgan." Gabe groaned and pressed his forehead against his forearms which were folded over the toilet seat.

"I wasn't asking if I fucked somebody else, Sunshine. I was referring to our true identities."

"Oh, that," I said casually. "Nah, you stayed in your role well.

Of course, Henry and George were far more hammered than you were, so it's not likely they'd remember."

"What about the ladies, Georgia and Petunia?"

I shouldn't have laughed at my husband when he was so obviously miserable, but I couldn't help it. "Her name is Petal, not Petunia. And no; they never returned downstairs."

"You clearly stayed sober, so did you learn anything juicy?"

"Does your dick wake up happy to see me when you're not hungover?"

Gabe reached down and cupped his junk. "Still happy to see you. I hope you won't be upset if I ignore him for now. I think my head might explode if we have sex."

"It's normally the objective," I teased. Gabe moaned, and I decided to cut him some slack. "Okay, you're referring to the one on your shoulders. Let me help you." I poured water into the glass I brought into the bathroom with me then added a packet of Theraflu. I mixed the concoction with my fingers since I didn't have a spoon handy and grabbed the ibuprofen I set out for Gabe.

Gabe slowly raised his head and looked at me when I lowered myself beside him on the floor. "What's that?"

"Remedies. Don't question me."

I could tell he wanted to probe deeper into my offerings but didn't when he saw the look on my face. Gabe popped four ibuprofen tablets into his mouth and washed it down with the Theraflu. "Fuck! What did I just drink? Skunk piss?"

"Quit being so dramatic," I told him. "It was only Theraflu."

"I don't have the flu," Gabe protested.

"You have an upset stomach and body aches, right?" Gabe's whimper was answer enough. "Give it time to hit your system. Do you think you're well enough to lie in bed and let me massage your head?" Gabe lifted a brow. "The one on your shoulders that is about to explode."

"I can try."

He moved like he was eighty-five years old but eventually got comfortable resting on the pillow I placed on my lap. I started off massaging his temples in slow, gentle circles. "Would you like to hear what I learned about the two couples we've met so far?"

"Did Henry and George get all loose-lipped after they got deep into their cups?"

"It wasn't what they said, but how they acted toward each other, and what I witnessed when I helped them to their rooms."

Gabe lifted his head up. "Helped them to their rooms? Where the hell was I?" Gabe's handsome features scrunched up into an angry scowl. "Wait. I think I remember us singing 'I Will Survive' on our way up in the elevator."

"You sure did," I agreed. "There was no way in hell I would risk any of you walking up the steps in your condition."

"You dropped me off at our room first."

"Yes, then I helped George and Henry to their rooms which are located beside one another with a connecting door granting them access to one another's rooms."

"Huh," Gabe said. "How do you know that?"

"I knocked on the door to the room George said was his, and Petal answered wearing a sheer negligee."

"The fuck you say."

"I don't think there was much fucking going on last night unless you count Petal and Georgia's romp before we came upstairs."

"Get out of here."

"Georgia was also in the room just as scantily clad. Petal stood back from the door, and I could see the connecting door between the rooms was open. Henry staggered into the room and said, 'Looks like the party is here tonight, Georgie Boy.' I kid you not, Gabe, he sniffed the air and yelled, 'I smell sex! You started the party without us. Again.' George stumbled into the room but didn't get far before he grabbed a big handful of Petal's breast. I worried he was going to pull her top down and expose her to my innocent eyes."

"What did the women say?" Gabe asked.

"Georgia put her hands on her hips and said, 'You two assholes expect us to wait up here and knit blankets while you're down there getting drunk?' And then Petal kissed George softly on the lips and removed his hand from her breast before she said, 'Tomorrow is a new day.' I knew something was up between the two couples, but I never would've guessed they were swingers?"

"Swingers? Like dancers?"

"Not swing dancers, Gabe. Swingers! Haven't you been listening to a word I've said? The two couples swap."

Gabe blinked a few seconds. "So, Georgia hooks up with Henry, and Petal hooks up with George." A few more blinks while he tried to work things out in his head. "Petal also hooks up with Georgia."

"Yes, and George and Henry appeared to be quite intimate as well. I saw lingering glances, and Henry squeezed George's thigh in a very familiar way."

"Wow," Gabe said. "I mean, I've heard of couples switching up or adding thirds, but I've never come across it in real life. It feels like we've landed in one of Chaz's books."

"I've already messaged him and planted the seed in his brain. Anyway, I couldn't get either man to confirm how long they've known each other. I did get Henry to admit he and Petal aren't brother and sister. George confessed it was just part of the roles they've chosen for the vacation. I do think they're as wealthy as they appear. George's boxers cost at least a hundred bucks a pair."

"Whoa! How the hell do you know that?" Gabe sat up too fast and gripped his head and stomach when his pain intensified.

"The drunken fool started pulling off his clothes before I could get the damn door shut. I tell you, I don't think they care who knows they're fucking each other. To be honest, I think they would've gone at it with me standing there."

"Pack your shit; we're going home," Gabe groused. I thought

his surly mood was adorable.

"Don't be silly, Gabe. Their romantic activities don't impact our lives one bit. How would you feel if guests refused to stay here because they didn't want to sleep under the same roof as gay men?"

"That's different," Gabe argued. "We're not shoving our sexy time in their faces. We've..."

His words trailed off when he realized anyone walking on the beach could've surmised we were making love on top of the lighthouse even if the concrete wall blocked them from actually seeing Gabe penetrate me. There was also the time we made love on our balcony in the rain. The wooden rail slats were close together, but I'm sure someone driving up in front of the house could've had an eyeful if they looked close enough. We weren't exactly discreet either.

"Okay, we're not leaving," Gabe said. "This better not be a fucking swinger's convention or some shit. I don't want to be fighting people off you for the duration of our stay."

"Nor I you, so we'll play it by ear. Let's agree to leave if things do get out of control or we feel uncomfortable."

"Agreed," Gabe said. He lay back down so I could massage his temples some more before I slid my fingers in his silky strands of hair and rubbed his scalp. "Your remedies are working wonders on my body," he told me about fifteen minutes later. "In fact, there's only one thing hurting me now."

"It's really hard to miss the flag pole waving in the air," I said. "You sure you're really up for it?"

"I can't believe you doubt me. You know what cures a headache, right?"

"A nap?"

"An orgasm followed by a nap. What time is it anyway?"

"I think it was about six o'clock when you jumped out of bed and ran to the bathroom. It's probably getting close to seven now."

"Yep, orgasm then a nap."

I gently eased out from under Gabe's head with the intention of kissing a path down his body to give him a blow job, but I saw his eyes were closed and he'd already drifted to sleep. I lay back down beside him to attempt to sleep rather than get up to do yoga or read. I doubted the other two couples would be making their way down to the gathering areas anytime soon, so it wouldn't hurt me to rest a little longer so I could stay sharp later.

Next thing I knew, Gabe was kissing me awake, and the delicious smell of pasta and garlic bread permeated the air. "Pierre makes his own pasta," my husband whispered in my ear. "How does fettuccine Alfredo with grilled chicken and broccoli sound to you? Juliette even sent up a few extra breadsticks for us."

"Is there a salad?" I asked. I couldn't eat such heavy food without trying to eat some fresh greens too.

"Yes, made with fresh produce from Pierre's garden. He even makes his own croutons and creamy Parmesan salad dressing."

I sat up when I heard the admiration in my husband's voice. "Don't let me catch you in the kitchen cozying up to Pierre."

"I'm not going into his kitchen," Gabe said, "but you are."

"Excuse me?"

"To make up for my failed date, Juliette helped me arrange for you to be his sous chef for a few hours tomorrow."

"Me? Work with a chef of his caliber?" I was equally excited and terrified. I could learn so much from him, or I could make an ass of myself.

"You get to help Pierre prepare a special dinner."

I just sat blinking at him. Was I still dreaming? I reached over to pinch him, but Gabe rolled out of the way.

"I don't think so, Sunshine. You're not dreaming, so there's no need to pinch anyone."

I cupped his face and kissed his lips. "Thank you for such a thoughtful gift."

"You're very welcome. Our family will reap the benefits of all you learn from him."

"Have you been downstairs yet, or did you order room service? What the hell time is it?"

"It's almost noon, and I've only been awake myself long enough to shower and order lunch. I figured I would venture down after you had a chance to eat and shower. Do you know what finally woke me up from my nap?"

"Your dick?"

"Surprisingly, no. It was the sound of additional guests arriving."

"Why didn't you lead with that part?" I asked, hopping from the bed and heading over to where the food waited in covered dishes to be devoured. "I think trying to figure out the other competitors is even more exciting than the mystery itself."

"The murder mystery starts the day after tomorrow, so I wouldn't be surprised if most of the competitors show up today. That way they can rest tomorrow after traveling and hit the ground running on Friday."

"Hit the ground running?" I asked. "It sounds like we've been cast as characters in a horror film."

Gabe laughed wickedly, earning a narrow look from me. I hated to watch horror movies, I sure as fuck didn't want to reenact one. Lucky for him, he was saved by an incoming FaceTime call from his mother.

I moved to sit closer to him on the couch, and he answered the call. "Hello, babies," I said when Dylan and Destiny came into view sitting on their grandmothers' laps. "Daddy and Papa miss you so much."

"Daddy! Papa!" Destiny said, reaching for the iPad Martina used to call us.

"Let Mamaw hold it for you, sweet girl," Martina said.

Destiny scrunched up her face just like Gabe when he's trying not to fart. I could tell she was about to throw a fit and needed a distraction, so I started singing "Isn't She Lovely?" She had no idea what the lyrics meant, but she clapped happily every time one of us sang it to her. It worked because she started to giggle and clap. Dylan looked back and forth between us like we both needed medication. At least until Gabe joined in, and then he thought it was the best thing ever. Dylan threw his head back and laughed heartily as only babies can do. Our mothers laughed too while Gabe and I continued to act like fools. It was okay because we were two fools in love with each other, our babies, and life.

After our song was over, we chatted for a while longer. Modern technology made it so much easier for us to be apart. I could see their little faces and hear their voices. If only I could smell their baby shampoo through FaceTime too.

"We're about to go swimming now that lunch has had a chance to settle in their tummies," my mom said.

"Grandmas will need a nap too," Martina added. "You guys go and enjoy your day. We'll talk to you later."

We blew air kisses and said how much we loved everyone before disconnecting. Gabe pulled the silver domed lids off our plates, and I was happy to see our entrées were still hot. "Keeping the salad in a separate chilled bowl is a nice touch," Gabe said. "I don't like a wilted salad."

"Let's dig in so we can check out the newest arrivals."

"I was thinking…" Gabe trailed off to take a huge bite of pasta.

"Yes?"

"Would you like to forget about the competition and go on a horseback ride or perhaps ride the jet skis on the river?"

"I think that sounds perfect, Gabe. Besides, we'll have plenty of time to meet the other couples at dinner."

Forty minutes later, we walked downstairs to Juliette's office to make arrangements for one of the activities, but she wasn't in her office. "Have you seen Juliette?" Gabe asked the young man behind the counter. According to his name tag, the guy was named Brandon.

"She took Bonnie and Clyde on a brief tour," he replied. "Juliette shouldn't be gone long."

"Bonnie and Clyde?" I asked, doing my best not to roll my eyes.

"Do you know them?" Brandon asked.

"They have the same names as infamous bank robbers from many years ago," Gabe told him. "Those aren't names you often hear anymore, and seldom as a pair."

"Oh, I guess it was before my time."

"It was before ours too." I refrained from pointing out that only knowing about current events set a dangerous precedence, but I let it go. "We'll just grab a drink and wait for Juliette."

"Sure thing," Brandon said cheerfully. "I'll tell her you were looking for her. What're your names?"

"Abbot and Costello," I replied. Brandon took out a message pad and started to write. "I was teasing, Brandon. Our names are Josh and Gabe."

"I am never drinking again," Gabe said.

"We can just grab a soda."

"I'm suddenly more interested in Bonnie and Clyde than I am riding horses," Gabe confessed.

"Me too. Let's not be obvious about it though. Or maybe we should. They wouldn't expect much different from a pole dancer and a professor."

"Too true. You're damned good at this, Sunshine."

"I'm good at most things," I reminded him.

"Touché."

TWELVE

Gabe

"What's this thing called again?" I asked Josh, buttoning my shirt. My voice was a mixture of exhaustion from our late-afternoon sex aerobics session and annoyance from having to dress up on vacation. Why couldn't we order in and watch television or sit on our balcony all night long? I wasn't even aware I'd packed a dress shirt. Oh right. Josh had packed a "just in case" suitcase.

"It's just some kind of social mixer where we can get to know the other participants who will also be trying to solve the mystery this weekend. We don't have to stay long. We'll eat dinner and be cordial then sneak away at the first opportunity." My husband's voice was calm and nonchalant which means he had a plan and it would be many hours before we made it back up to our room. I also knew he'd make it up to me when we did, so I went along with it rather than calling him out. I referred to this as picking my battles. A person only had so much energy to expend, and he'd sucked and fucked nearly all of mine out of me. I wouldn't waste what was left on arguing.

"Remember, you need to act angry at me for something. We want the competition to see us as weak. What?" Josh asked when he looked over at me.

"I didn't say anything."

"Your furrowed brow and scowling eyes are saying a lot," Josh countered.

"I just don't want our fake fighting to turn into real fighting," I answered. "This never works in television or movies. Someone always says some passive-aggressive remark to get a dig in at the other person then tries to scoff it off as part of their act."

"Babe, passive aggressive isn't my forte. I'm very upfront with my scorn and derision."

"One could argue your snarkiness is the epitome of passive-aggressive behavior," I countered.

Josh turned away fully from the mirror he'd been looking into while styling his hair. I knew the hands on his hips, tilted head, and narrowed eyes meant he was working his way into righteous—or unrighteous—indignation. I learned a very long time ago never to refer to it as a hissy fit because it fueled the first fight we ever had and almost destroyed us before we had a chance to get started.

"You knew you were marrying a snarkicist," Josh said. "I believe you were the one who invented the phrase."

"I did," I replied, nodding. "I also seem to remember defining the term as someone who uses snark as a main form of communication, often in a passive-aggressive way. And yes, I married you in all of your snark glory, and I wouldn't change a single thing about you, Josh. All I'm saying is: I do not want our fake fight turning into a real fight."

"It won't," Josh said certainly.

I wish I could feel as certain as he was, but I had a strange feeling his plans would go sideways or blow up in our faces. All I could do was remain calm, remind myself to play the role of professor, and remember it was only a game.

"You are so damn delicious, husband of mine," Josh said as he walked over to the suitcase holding our costumes. "I'm just going to borrow a few things from here so you can look the part of a professor." I was too distracted by his sexy ass when he bent over to open the luggage for his words to penetrate my mind right away.

"How do you know what I packed?" I asked.

"I fucked you into a stupor then searched your suitcase to make sure you didn't pack lame costumes," Josh said, turning to look over his shoulder at me. "How's that for honesty?"

"Lame costumes?" I asked incredulously. "You think I'm lame?"

"Poor word choice," Josh said then turned back to the suitcase. "I should've said costumes that weren't up to my standards."

"You think I don't know how picky you are by now?" I challenged.

"Picky?" Josh asked. "I prefer the word particular. I'm very particular about everything in my life. I have to admit you went above and beyond with our costumes. I didn't think it was possible for me to love and respect you more than I already did. You upped the ante here." Josh straightened and turned to face me. He held a suede jacket with patches sewn on the elbows and a pipe. "Fucking genius, Sherlock."

I stood taller after hearing his high praise. "The Sherlock props are actually for you. There's also a hat just like his. I was planning to go as Watson."

Josh looked at the jacket in his hand. "I guess a doctor might wear a jacket like this too, but a stuffy professor definitely would. You did good, babe."

"Well, I didn't predict you'd need a mesh belly shirt and spandex shorts to parade around in to play up your role."

"Please, your love has changed me. I'm a stay-at-home dad now. I mean, on occasion, the old me might surface when needed."

"You better watch what parts of you surface, Sunshine. I'm not going to pretend we're swingers to win a game."

"I'd never ask you to, babe. That's taking things too far even for me."

Josh's casual, stay-at-home-dad look meant he could get by with a simple button-up shirt. I, on the other hand, was forced to wear a blazer in July long enough to make an impression. I was sure a sweat-drenched dress shirt would make a really nice impression. Luckily, we were the last of the six couples to show up for dinner and a show, as Josh called it. I planned to take my jacket off as soon as we sat down to dinner, and I had no intention of putting it back on again.

"I must admit, Bonnie and Clyde play their roles well," Josh whispered. "Those period outfits and suspicious scowls are a nice touch."

"I can't tell if their distant attitudes are part of their roles or their personality," I told him.

"We'll find out."

"Indeed."

In addition to Bonnie and Clyde, Mitzi and her daughter, Candace, and Laurel and her cousin, Yanny, showed up. Josh snorted when he overheard the latter team introduce themselves to another couple when they arrived earlier in the day. I had no idea what the hell he found so funny until we returned to our room to get ready for dinner.

"How can anyone listen to the recording and hear anything other than Yanny?" I'd asked.

"Because it's Laurel," he had responded. I'd heard Laurel too, but I wanted to rile him up. I might not be on social media, but plenty of officers talked about the Laurel and Yanny debate. Hell, even Ellen discussed it on her show. I didn't immediately make the connection like Josh did. My decision to yank his chain worked and resulted in our afternoon sex aerobics.

I thought I would look ridiculously out of place, but Mitzi would've taken the grand prize had it been a contest. "I hope the fur coat is fake," I whispered.

"Cruella is a bit over the top, isn't she? Who do you suppose she's trying to be? Aged Hollywood starlet?"

"Something like that," I agreed. "I can't decide about Candace. I think she plays the vapid young starlet very well, but there's shrewdness in her gaze. I'd watch her if I were you, Sunshine. I think she's our stiffest competition."

"Oh good! Everyone is here now, so we can get started," Juliette announce excitedly. All eyes turned to us.

The conspiring wink George shot at me said "atta boy" while the rest of the group sized us up. I could tell it was a competitive, cutthroat crowd. I felt the energy radiating off my husband as he held up his hand and wiggled his fingers in a cute wave.

"My apologies, everyone. I misplaced my pipe, and I do enjoy a good smoke after dinner. Shall we begin?"

"Absolutely," Juliette replied with a smile, gesturing for Josh and me to take a seat at one of the tables.

I wasn't in the mood for any of the swingers' shenanigans, so I guided Josh over to the table where Bonnie and Clyde sat. They both looked shocked that their "stay away" expressions failed to work.

"Good evening," I said to them, pulling out a chair for Josh before sitting beside him. It seemed like the proper thing to do in my new role. It must've worked because Josh squeezed my thigh under the table.

Bonnie gave the barest nod in greeting while Clyde continued to scowl at us. I figured it was good practice for how our kids will look at us when they're hormonal teenagers.

"Tonight is all about getting to know one another," Juliette said from the front of the room. "We'll eat the special dinner Chef Pierre prepared for us then we'll play some games."

Mitzi snorted. "Games? As in Monopoly?"

"Not exactly," Juliette answered calmly in the face of derision. "After dinner, you'll all have some drinks at the bar while we set up the activities."

"Activities?" Petal asked in her baby-soft voice. "Sounds promising."

"Not *your* kind of activities," Clyde mumbled, but it was loud enough for people sitting at our table to hear. I wanted to fist-bump the guy, but he didn't return the wry smile I aimed at him, so I kept my fist to myself.

"Six couples are participating this weekend, so we are going to set up several activity tables where you'll sit across from another couple and participate together. Now, you won't have to attend all the tables, but I do expect you to interact with all of the couples." She looked right at our table when she made the last remark, so I knew she must've addressed it to Bonnie and Clyde. We'd never given her reason to suspect we wouldn't socialize with others, so it had to be a conclusion she drew after the private tour she gave them of Tarlington House. "I'm going to set a timer, and when it goes off, you'll either get up and move to a different table or wait there to meet a different couple using an activity you feel comfortable with. We do ask that you keep the activities to just two couples at a time.

"Does anyone have any questions?" No one spoke up, so she gave the group a firm nod. "It's time to eat the special feast laid out for you then." She gestured to the table laden with sterling silver serving dishes.

I reminded myself to walk and act suave when what I wanted to do was lower my shoulder and ram anyone who got between me and the delicious-smelling food. Pierre went all out with this, and I was even more excited about Josh spending time with him the following afternoon. I had a hard time choosing between the delicious prime rib or the scrumptious-looking seafood.

"I don't think you have to choose," Josh said when he caught my gaze volleying back and forth between the cuts of prime rib he uncovered and the lobster tails I discovered beneath the lid in my hand. "I think you can have a slice of prime rib and eat a lobster tail. Oh look," he said excitedly. "There are king crab legs too, and I think Petal just lifted a lid to reveal lobster bisque."

"Nobody makes rice pilaf like Pierre," George purred.

Josh and I looked down the long table to observe the older couple.

"Oh joy!" Georgia responded with fake enthusiasm. "Garlic breath."

"I'm sure the amount of alcohol you plan to consume will burn your nostrils enough to lessen the impact."

"George has serious snark game," Josh said in awe. "This is the best vacation, babe." He stepped around me to inch closer to the feuding couple who continued to argue but at a much lower volume. Josh couldn't allow that.

"Are you going to take a lobster tail or are you just going to stand there with the lid so they get cold and are ruined for everyone else?"

I turned to face Clyde. I wanted to smash the heavy lid into his face to wipe the indignant look away. Instead, I cocked my brow like a snooty professor unaccustomed to having someone like him address me directly. "I believe it is *I*, the professor, who should be schooling *you* on propriety and manners, not the other way around."

"Oh, you sound like the headmaster at my boarding school," Bonnie said, peering at me from beneath her lashes. "So strict and well-spoken."

"Move along, strumpet," Petal said fervently. "He's a happily married man who doesn't play around, especially with the likes of you."

"*Me?* That's rich coming from *you.*"

"You look smug for someone who pretends her brother is her gun-toting, bank-robbing lover."

Bonnie threw her head back and laughed. "How is that any different than what you do? At least we're not fucking. Do you call him brother when he's—"

Petal's fist came from nowhere and smashed into Bonnie's nose before she screamed, "You jealous little shrew! Maybe you should've tried making him happier."

Bonnie wiped the blood leaking from her nose with the back of her hand. "He was perfectly happy until you came along with your debauched lifestyle. We were going to get married and have a family."

"His balls were drying up every second he spent engaged to you. It was only a matter of time before they shriveled up and fell off."

Bonnie let out a war cry and launched herself at Petal. They tumbled to the ground and began yanking hair and swinging fists as they battled for dominance and traded barbs.

"Couldn't get it up for you…"

"Surprised it hasn't fallen off from disease…"

"Maybe if you knew your ass could hold more than your angry stick…"

"Faithless whore…"

Normally, my reaction time was quicker, but I was shocked by the uncouth display. Not Josh. He jumped right into the fray along with Henry and separated the clawing, screaming women.

"I guess you're not used to seeing such vulgarities, are you, teach?" Clyde asked, shaking his head. "I don't know what she's ever seen in him, or why she can't let him go."

I followed his line of sight, expecting him to be looking at his sobbing sister who was being consoled by Henry, but he was looking at Petal who leaned against Georgia's ample bosom.

"The heart wants what the heart wants. There's no use fighting it," I said, sounding like a pompous, philosophical professor.

Josh came to me then, wrapped his arms around my bicep, and tugged me away while everyone sorted themselves out. "I'm impressed you were able to suppress your cop instincts to stay in your professor role, babe."

"Honestly, it caught me completely by surprise, and I was slow to react. I think I've gotten too soft."

Josh snickered. "That's *never* been an issue."

I straightened his crooked shirt and ran my finger over the dangling threads that used to secure a button to the top. "You lost a button in the scuffle. You're a natural at breaking up fights."

"It's an unfortunate skill, and one I haven't had to use often." Sadness washed over his face, and I knew he was thinking about the last time he saw his friend Georgia in his salon. She'd gotten in a big fight with her ex-husband's new wife and had words with Josh afterward. Georgia Beaumont might've been a difficult person, but he loved her and always regretted that she died before they could make up. "Let's just hope this catfight doesn't end with another Georgia's death."

I glanced up and caught Bonnie glaring at Georgia across the expanse of the room. There was definitely bad blood between them too.

"Excuse me, everyone," Juliette said. "In light of what just happened, I'm afraid I have to ask you all to return upstairs. You can place your dinner orders, and we'll deliver to your rooms. We don't accept this kind of behavior at Tarlington House, so we will be conducting meetings with the parties involved in tonight's altercation."

There was grumbling and more heated barbs exchanged between the sparring women, but they were kept separate for the most part as we all made our way up the grand staircases. I thought it was a good idea Bonnie took the steps on the right while Petal took the staircase on the left.

"So, what the hell happened?" Josh asked once we were alone. I gave him the rundown, and he whistled when I finished. "Bonnie and Clyde are brother and sister pretending to be lovers. They *are* pretending, right?" I just shrugged because I had no way of knowing. "And Henry and Petal are lovers pretending to be siblings." I nodded. "And there's some love triangle between Petal, Bonnie, and Henry?"

"I think Clyde is in love with Petal."

"This is the best vacation ever. I think Chaz could write at least two or three books out of this fuckery. Damn, baby. You sure know how to pick them."

"I sure do," I said, looking at my beautiful, smiling man.

THIRTEEN

Josh

As usual, Gabe easily drifted off to sleep after a late dinner and heart-pounding sex. I had hoped the full belly and orgasm would help me fall asleep too, but I wasn't as fortunate. I lay there, willing my brain to shut the fuck up, but it wasn't cooperating. There was no fucking way I was leaving our suite to explore the inn with so much going on, so I got out of bed and grabbed the paperback copy of *What Alice Forgot* by Liane Moriarty I purchased the prior week after several of my clients couldn't stop talking about it when they sat in my chair.

It seemed Maegan's small book club at Books and Brew had expanded because nearly every customer in our salon was talking about the same book. The premise of the book sounded interesting, and I felt like it was a book anyone could relate to. A lady goes to the gym to work out, falls off her spinning bike, and knocks herself out. When she comes to, she thinks the year is 1998 instead of 2008. In her mind, she was on the verge of having her first child with the husband she adored, but in reality, she had three children and was about to get divorced. Alice lost ten years of her life. She couldn't remember giving birth to her children, and she couldn't come to grips with the fact her marriage was over. It was just unfathomable to her that there would be a day when she didn't love Nick. He was her everything.

I flipped on the reading lamp beside the overstuffed, wingback chair and snuggled in with the throw blanket that was artfully arranged across the chair. I expected to enjoy the book, but I didn't anticipate just how captivated I would become. My eyes devoured each word on every page I turned, my heart squeezing tighter in my chest as Alice's memories returned to her in little fragments. My eyes became tired after a few hours, but I fought off sleepiness to keep reading. Just one more chapter. Then tears washed the gritty feeling from my eyes as I put myself in Alice's shoes and tried to imagine how it would feel to forget the past ten years of my life. A kaleidoscope of beautiful images rushed through my mind. Meeting Gabe, hating Gabe, falling head over heels in love with Gabe, committing my life to Gabe, and bringing home our babies with Gabe. He was the fucking center of my universe, and everything revolved around him.

I looked over several times to make sure my husband was still sleeping soundly in the bed, and I hadn't imagined his existence. It was silly, but some books punch you in the gut. They make you think and yearn and feel. I wanted to keep reading to find out what happened between Alice and Nick, but my need to feel Gabe's warmth and hear his heart beating within his chest was stronger. I gently laid the book on the end table like it was a priceless treasure, turned off the light, and returned to bed.

"Where'd you go?" Gabe asked sleepily when I burrowed beneath his arm to rest my head on his chest. I closed my eyes and just listened to his steady heartbeat for a few seconds.

"Australia," I replied.

"Without me? How rude. I hope you remembered to wear sunscreen."

"It's winter in Australia right now," I told him.

"Huh. I didn't know that," Gabe said before drifting back to sleep.

"I love you so fucking much, Gabe." His arm tightened around me in response. My brain tried to fire back up with thoughts about what I'd read and predictions on how the story ended, but I was able to block them and fall asleep.

"Wake up, sleepyhead," Gabe whispered in my ear. "You've got a big day ahead of you."

"Oh, yeah?" I asked, reaching for him. Gabe leaped off the bed suddenly to avoid my touch. It woke me up quicker than if he'd dumped a bucket of ice water on me. I scowled when I realized he stood a few feet from the bed. "What's wrong?"

"Nothing is wrong," he assured me. "I just know what happens if you get your skilled hands on my body."

"That's a bad thing?"

"It is when you're pressed for time," Gabe replied. "I don't want you to be late."

"Late for what?" Then I realized what was significant about the day. I could tell by the brightness in the room it was much later than my usual hour to wake up. "What time is it?" I asked.

"It's eleven o'clock."

"In the morning?" I shrieked. "Gabe! Don't I need to meet Pierre at noon?"

"Twelve thirty."

"I need to take a shower and wake the fuck up."

"Brunch first," Gabe told me, gesturing to the silver domes in the sitting area. "How does an omelet, hash browns, fruit, and toast sound to you? There's even a French vanilla cappuccino for you."

"You're so thoughtful, and I adore you." As soon as I spoke, memories of the angst I'd felt while reading flooded my brain. "I can't imagine a day without you." Then I promptly burst into tears, scaring the hell out of my husband.

"Sunshine, what's wrong?"

I told him about the book in jagged fragments between sniffles, sobs, and hiccups. "I don't want to wake up and forget our wedding or the beauty of holding our babies against our chest during our skin-to-skin bonding. I told myself, 'Josh, don't be silly. It's just a book.' People have accidents and lose their memories though, Gabe. Or what if I end up with Alzheimer's someday?"

"Oh, Sunshine," Gabe said, pressing my head against his shoulder. "Life is full of *what if*, so we better spend our energy on the *right now*." I nodded because I knew he was right. "Let's start with breakfast then you can shower, and we can call home before you have to meet with Pierre."

"Sounds perfect."

I felt a thousand times better after eating, showering, and reading a quick story to them. Seeing our babies blow kisses at us made everything better. I set my anxiety over Alice's predicament aside so I could put my full attention on not making an ass of myself in Pierre's kitchen.

"Don't be nervous, Sunshine. You're going to do great," Gabe said when we stood outside Juliette's door waiting for her to finish a call. "Furthermore, I bet you'll have a lot of fun."

"Not if he's like Gordon Ramsey."

"Who's that?" Gabe inquired.

"The blond chef who screams profanities at people," I told him. "I know you've seen the previews for his show."

"I somehow doubt Geneva Louderback would employ a kitchen tyrant like him."

"You're right," Juliette said. "Pierre is a sweet teddy bear of a man. He's also a genius in the kitchen. He doesn't need to yell and scream to earn respect. You'll see what I'm talking about."

I felt better after hearing Juliette's assurance. "What will you do, Gabe?"

"I think I'll go read the final chapter in your book so I can taunt you later."

I dramatically gasped and covered my heart. "You wouldn't!"

"I'm surprised you didn't think of it already. I seem to recall a confession that you used to flip to the last page of a book to make sure it had a happy ending."

"You didn't?" Juliette asked, sounding as appalled as I did just a few seconds prior. "It ruins the story."

"Not if you're too anxious to enjoy the story in the first place," I told her before shifting my attention back to my husband. "As tempted as I was, Chaz broke me of the habit once he started publishing books."

"Why were you tempted with this book?" Juliette asked me.

"This author is new to me, and I'm not sure if I can trust her with my heart yet," I replied. "I know some of my favorite authors will cut my heart into a thousand pieces during a story, but I also know they will sew it back together by the end. I don't know if Miss Liane can be trusted."

"Josh, you are so damn adorable," Juliette said, pinching my cheek like one of my great-aunts used to do when I was a kid. I wasn't trying to be adorable though; I was telling the truth. Miss

Liane Moriarty needed to earn my trust, only time and one hundred and twenty two pages would tell. "Are you ready?"

"As I'll ever be," I replied.

After a quick kiss with Gabe, I followed Juliette through the employee entrance and passageways until we reached the kitchen. A tall, beautiful black man with a joyful smile stood in the center of the room.

"You must be Josh," he said, stepping forward to shake my hand. His French Creole accent made his words flow smoothly like satin.

"It is such an honor to spend time with you in your kitchen," I said.

"We're happy to have you here," Pierre said. "Ready to get started?"

"I am."

"Wash station is over there, grab an apron, and then we're going to have a meeting and go over assignments for the day. Do you have any food allergies I need to know about?"

"No, sir."

"Great. Let's get started." He gestured toward the wash station that was separate from the sink they used to wash and prep food.

I thoroughly scrubbed my hands before rinsing and drying them. Pierre patiently waited for me to grab an apron and return to the center of the room. All the sous chefs had stopped what they were doing at their stations to join him. Pierre made quick introductions around the room before passing out a very detailed menu for the elaborate dinner he planned. He broke down each course and everyone's responsibility for the course. I was impressed by his demeanor and humor when a few of the chefs groaned about their assigned tasks.

"If you are lucky, Josh will assist you on that course," he'd say.

"Happy to," I assured the chefs.

"Let's get to it then," Pierre said, clapping his hands to get everyone pumped up. He headed off to the wash station to prep for his day.

I followed Donna to her workstation since she was prepping the first course. She was tasked with making a Greek-inspired salad and had expressed dread for pitting olives and working with anchovies. I'd never pitted olives before, but I was eager to learn.

"Normally you can pit them by placing a large knife flat against the olive and pressing firmly down with your other hand."

"Oh, it's how I peel garlic," I said enthusiastically.

"It's the fastest way, but Chef doesn't like to serve mangled olives in his salads. He likes to serve them whole."

"I understand; it looks more appealing whole," I told her.

Donna picked up a metal tool with her right hand and an olive with her left. She placed the olive in a circular opening at the bottom of the tool then squeezed her right hand. The top of the tool pierced the flesh of the olive and pushed the pit out through the bottom. Donna released the tool and held up the pitted olive for me to inspect. "Perfectly intact and pitted. That's what we're looking for."

"I can do this," I assured her. "How many?"

Donna gestured to the two containers holding olives. "Both of these containers because I will be putting some of them in the salad dressing also." No wonder she hated pitting olives. The tedious task would eat into her prep time.

"I got you covered."

It took me a dozen or so before I found my rhythm. I was afraid to press too hard and squish the flesh, but too soft meant the tool got stuck halfway through the olive. Once I learned the right pressure and technique, I sailed through the task. Then Donna showed me how to prepare the anchovies for the salad and how much to set aside for the dressing.

After I finished helping her, I moved over to Dana's station. "Was my sister nice to you?" she asked.

"Very," I replied. "How can I help?"

"Have you ever had gazpacho before?" she asked. I shook my head. "It's a very simple cold soup with hundreds of variations. Today, we're making Thai-infused gazpacho. I've already cut the yellow tomatoes, but can you cut half of these cucumbers and yellow bell peppers into one-inch chunks and dice these shallots?"

"I'd be glad to."

After I finished, Dana dumped the vegetables in a large food processor to begin breaking them down. Then she added the seasonings and liquid and pureed it all together until smooth. She stuck a spoon down into the concoction then handed it to me. "What do you think?"

"Delicious," I told her. "I'm going to make it at home."

"We'll refrigerate this so it gets nice and cold then add a swirl of coconut milk on top and a spicy grilled shrimp in the center."

"I can't wait."

I kept moving down the line, helping Bruce, Ned, Stacey, and Max, until I reached Pierre who hadn't even broken a sweat as he calmly worked. "By now, you can tell I've chosen an international theme for dinner tonight."

I most certainly could. Pierre chose foods from every corner of the world to serve his guests. "You sure are passionate about your job."

"I need to cook as other people need to breathe," Pierre said. "Tonight's main entrée is beef Wellington. It looks like such a simple dish but getting a perfect puff pastry that isn't soggy on the bottom is very difficult. I refuse to use or serve pâté, so I'm going to wrap the tenderloin in a few layers of thinly sliced Parma ham. Then I add a mixture of mushrooms and roasted chestnuts to act as a barrier to keep the juices from seeping out and making my pastry soggy. I had to make my puff pastry in advance, but you can help me roll it out if you'd like."

"Absolutely." I paid rapt attention as I watched Pierre work the pastry like a magician. "I want to be just like you when I grow up."

He chuckled. "It just takes practice. Let's see what you got?"

Pierre supervised and guided me through the first one then left me alone to work on the others. When I finished, I helped him wrap the tenderloins with Parma ham and spread the mushroom and roasted chestnut paste all around the meat.

"This is the tricky part," he told me. "We need to wrap the tenderloin tight so air pockets won't form between the meat and pastry when it puffs up. I will demonstrate for you."

He made it look so damn easy. I would need steady hands to make sure I didn't overwork the pastry, or it would ruin the texture. Pierre patiently guided me through the first one then stood back and watched me wrap the remaining tenderloins in pastry.

"You're a natural," he said when I finished. "Are you ready to help with dessert?"

"Absolutely. What country are we representing with dessert?"

"America, and nothing symbolizes us better than apple pie." He cocked a brow when a wry smile spread across my face. "I can see it pleases you."

"I'm famous for my apple pies where I come from."

"Tell me what makes your pies special, Josh," Pierre said.

"Bourbon."

"I've met my kindred spirit," Pierre said. "I'll go raid the bar while you peel and slice apples."

"Deal," I said.

I couldn't wait to see Gabe's expression when he tasted the food I helped make. I giggled when I imagined him trying to confiscate everyone's pie or finagle an entire pie for himself. When Pierre returned, he held a bottle of top-shelf liquor in his hand.

"This do?"

"Oh yeah. That is sure to help lighten everyone's mood so we avoid another clash like the one from last night."

Booze and bitter rivals. What could go wrong?

FOURTEEN

Gabe

Josh arrived back at our room flushed, glowing, and slightly sweaty. For a split second, I was worried about what happened in the kitchen with Chef Pierre and jealous I wasn't the one who put that smile on his face.

"Best. Gift. Ever!" Josh said then launched himself into my arms. Okay, maybe I was behind the smile after all. "I learned so much, and I had an amazing time. I can't wait to tell you all about it, but I have to hurry up and shower so we won't be late for dinner."

Josh pulled his shirt off over his head and dropped it on the floor before removing the rest of his clothes and shoes. "You should come keep me company." My husband shot me a playful wink before he turned and walked to the bathroom. Would I ever get tired of seeing that perfect ass? Hell no.

"I thought you didn't want to be late."

"I meant you could sit on the toilet lid or lean against the bathroom vanity and chat with me while I rush through my routine. We might need to rehearse a little too. I think we should have a big fight and let these people think they can divide us."

The mere thought made my heart ache. I loved that we didn't fight and argue very often, and our home was happy and harmonious. Slinging insults, even if they were only pretend, just felt so damn wrong to me. "What do you want to fight about?"

"Let's make it something OTP that wouldn't normally cause a knock-down, drag-out fight."

"OTP?" I asked.

"Over the top," Josh replied, stepping into the shower. "I forget that you don't speak in acronyms as the rest of us do."

"Over the top, huh? Do you mean like asking me to sit here and watch you shower and not touch you or myself?"

Josh whipped his head around and stared at me through the glass. "Do you want to touch yourself right now, Gabe?"

"I'd rather touch you, but as you pointed out, we don't have enough time to do the kind of touching we want."

"Hey, I'm quite fond of five-minute hand jobs or blow jobs when we're pressed for time," he said with a cute pout.

"I like them too, and sometimes it's necessary, but we're not in a hurry this week. We can come back here after dinner and take our sweet time making love."

"Or you can bring your sexy ass in here right now and make me scream."

My dick strained against my dress pants, but I was going to

ignore it and resist the urge to claim him. Then he turned around and seductively ran his soapy hands over his ass, parting his cheeks for me to have a good look before running his middle finger along the crack.

Fuck it! I launched myself off the vanity and walked straight into the shower, not caring about getting my clothes wet. I was determined to hold out and only focus on pleasuring him, but Josh wanted no part of that. He yanked my shirt open, sending buttons scattering all over the shower floor, and attacked my belt and pants.

My need to possess him clawed at my guts, but I would never willingly hurt him. Fast and hard didn't mean brutal and uncaring. I worked Josh open with lubed fingers while he sucked my tongue and stroked my cock. Once he was ready, I hoisted him up and pinned him against the tiled wall before I thrust home. Josh pulled my hair and bit my bottom lip, urging me to go faster and harder. I gave in to what we both wanted—needed—while only pulling my mouth off his long enough to nibble and suck on his neck.

Normally, I marked him where only I would see it, but I lost control when he dug his heels into my ass, spurring me on. Josh trembled in my arms and dug his fingers in my shoulders while chanting, "More. More. More." I fucked and sucked harder until we both came on a shout.

I lowered my head against his shoulder while he clung tight to my body. "You turn me into a rutting animal." Josh's response was a playful growl that made me laugh. I gently pulled out then lowered him to his feet. "Now we really need to hurry," I told him as I started to wash the lube and cum off my cock.

"Just leave the clothes in here for now," Josh said when I went to grab them. "We can lay them on the balcony to dry later. What'd you do today?"

I reached for the towel and began drying my body. "I lounged lazily on the balcony and read your book."

"What book?

"The one that made you so emotional."

"Alice?"

I chuckled because he made the book sound like a person. "Yep. I probably haven't gotten as far as you though, so don't ruin anything for me."

Josh snorted and turned off the shower. "I don't ruin books for you."

"'It was so sad when Joey was bitten by a zombie and had to be put down.' Sound familiar to you? I hadn't gotten to that part yet before you crushed me with the revelation. That was when I knew our two-person book club wasn't going to work."

"You sure do know how to hold a grudge," Josh grumbled while toweling off.

"You sure do know how to ruin a book."

"Will you ever let me live it down?" Josh asked softly.

"No, but I'll find a way to get my revenge."

"How?"

"I know how Alice ends," I tossed over my shoulder as I walked to the closet.

Josh gasped. "You didn't?"

"To be honest, I didn't intend to read the book. I just opened to the last page so I could tease you about the ending, but the last page made me want to read the entire last chapter, and that made me want to know how Alice got from knocked out on the gym floor to there. So, I started reading from the beginning. Next thing I knew, you were back from your big day with Chef Pierre."

"I'm telling Chaz you cheated," Josh said menacingly.

"Okay, but tell him after dinner. I want to see what made you so excited when you came back to our room."

"You just want to appease your second favorite organ now that your favorite one is satisfied…for the time being." He had a point. "We'll chat more about Alice later."

Josh wasn't too happy with me when he noticed the mark I

left on his neck just above his collarbone. "I guess it plays into our roles. I'm the hot, horny former pole dancer who corrupted you with private dances. You risked your academic career to be with me, and you like to remind me of it when we argue."

"I could work with that."

"If we fight over something really stupid, it will be obvious the tension has been building up between us for a long time. The little thing was finally what made us snap. I'll let you decide what silly thing annoys you and start the fight." Josh glanced at his watch. "Showtime. Give me one last sweet kiss before we go downstairs acting like we're irritated with one another."

"Remember not to let this fake fight turn into a real fight," I said after our kiss.

"Of course."

Everyone was already in the dining room when we arrived. I figured there was no time like the present to have a professorial fit about time management. "See," I said loudly, gesturing to the gathering crowd. I could feel their attention turn to me. "I told you we were going to be late. Again."

Josh blinked rapidly like my raised voice upset him. He swallowed hard then dramatically covered his hickey with his hand, calling everyone's attention to it. "I think you need to take some responsibility for your actions, dear." It wasn't possible for him to completely bury his snark. He winked playfully at someone then sauntered away with an extra sway in his hips. God, I loved him so damn much.

Clyde ambled over toward me. "Atta boy, teach." If he held up his fist for a bump, I would be tempted to *accidentally* miss and catch him in the mouth instead. "He's a spirited one."

"That he is."

"You seem like an odd pair if you don't mind me saying so. You're so masculine, and he's so…" He let his words trail off. "Well, you know." I knew I wanted him to shut the fuck up. Who the hell was this loser to judge us? He didn't know a fucking thing about us beyond what we let him see. "A bit flirty too, I'd say." Clyde nodded in the direction of where Josh stomped off to, but I was fully aware of where my husband stood in the room and who had taken advantage of our tiff to approach him. "That sly bastard Henry sure doesn't waste a minute, does he?"

"So it would seem," I said dryly.

"I'm sure you've nothing to worry about if that little mark you left on your man is an indication of your passionate nature."

"Stop trying to stir up trouble," Bonnie said, joining us. "There's plenty of it already." I noticed she was looking at Petal, Georgia, and George who were watching the interaction between Josh and Henry with hopeful expressions on their faces. "Whatever you do, do not get involved with those four. They won't stop until they destroy a beautiful relationship."

"How do you know?" Clyde asked snidely. "You wouldn't recognize a beautiful relationship if it kicked you in the teeth." I wanted to kick him in the teeth.

"Because, even now, they're so attuned to one another. Josh knows exactly where Gabe is in the room, and Gabe can barely tear his eyes away from his husband. Every few seconds, their gazes meet and hold. Their kind of passion and love can't be disguised."

"Sounds dreadful," Clyde said. "I can't imagine finding anyone who could hold my attention like that." I looked over and caught him watching Petal again.

"Best you cast your eyes in another direction, Brother. You don't want to get caught up in their seek-and-destroy games." Oh, I thought Clyde was eager to get snagged in their games. It seems Petal knew it too because she winked at him when she caught him watching her. You could feel the fury radiating off Bonnie after witnessing the exchange. She moved closer to her brother and lowered her voice just loud enough for Clyde and me to hear. "You'll be wise to stay away from her if you know what's good for you, my dear brother."

Clyde tore his eyes off of Petal long enough to look at his sister. "You can blame *Petal* for your failed relationship all you want, but she didn't force *Henry* to stray. He's a philandering asshole, and she did you a favor by revealing that to you before you married him."

"Oh ho," Bonnie loudly said, clasping her chest and taking a dramatic step back. "You think I should go over there and *thank* that slut for what she did? I should be grateful she pretended to be my friend while she fucked my fiancé? Are you so blinded by her looks you can't see the evil lurking beneath the glamorous façade?"

"I think you're once again acting overdramatic about something that happened years ago, Sister. Of course, I think what they did was wrong, but it's time to stop feeling sorry for yourself and move on. Find a nice man who wants the same things as you, and don't make this man pay for *Henry's* mistakes. All men aren't the same, and it's time you embrace that and move on."

"He's right," I said. "Well, about moving on and finding happiness. Life is too short to be so miserable." I leaned toward her and lowered my voice. "I've been told the best revenge is to get on with your life and be happy. Won't that drive Petal nuts when she sees she no longer has power over you?"

Bonnie tipped her head to the side as if she was considering my words. "I know you're right, Gabe. I've been stuck in this rut for so long I can't seem to find my way out."

"You start by deciding you're letting go of the pain, and you continue to take one step at a time," I told her. She smiled tentatively then inhaled deeply into her lungs, held the breath a few seconds, and slowly released it. Letting go of her anger wouldn't be quite that easy, but remembering to breathe was a good start. Damn, I sounded more and more like Josh every single day.

Clyde scoffed. "I've been saying this for years, but you haven't listened to me. Why him?"

"Because he doesn't want me to move past my grudge just so

he can fuck my enemy," Bonnie snarled. And just like that, the tenuous peace Bonnie had found was gone. I thought she might benefit by putting some distance between herself and Clyde as well.

I was saved by Juliette asking us to have a seat so dinner could be served. Then she announced we would participate in the activities that were canceled the previous night. A chorus of groans rang out from around the room. I thought Juliette was pushing things too far, but it wasn't my place to say anything to her.

Josh crossed the room and joined me at the table I chose. Surprisingly, Mitzi, Candace, Yanny, and Laurel joined us too.

"You seem the most normal," Candace said in a baby-soft voice. She wasn't dressed like Marilyn Monroe but sounded like her.

"I think Juliette should lock the four of them in a room and let them fight it or fuck it out of their systems," Yanny added.

"Ignore my cousin," Laurel said. "We don't let him out much, and he hasn't learned it's very crude to speak like that in public. This isn't the locker room at the gym. I'm very sorry." The apology seemed to be aimed at Mitzi and Candace.

"Cousins, huh?" Mitzi asked. "Real ones or kissing ones? We got siblings pretending to be lovers and lovers pretending to be siblings. Why not cousins who aren't really cousins." I looked across the room and saw the three remaining couples had put the expanse of the dining area between them. George, Georgia, Petal, and Henry sat at the same table while Clyde and Bonnie sat at a table by themselves. I actually felt sorry for Bonnie and would've invited them to join us, but our table only seated six people.

Yanny threw his head back and laughed. "I like you, Mitzi."

"We're truly cousins," Laurel said. "Oddly enough, our names really are Laurel and Yanny. We get teased mercilessly now since the audio clip came out."

"Seriously?" Josh asked, narrowing his eyes.

"Seriously," Yanny said. He pulled his wallet out and showed us his name was indeed Yannis which he shortened to Yanny.

"Would you like to see mine too?" Laurel asked. We declined because Yanny's name was more unbelievable than hers.

Throughout dinner, we chatted about our lives. I didn't know how much was true, but Mitzi looked and sounded like a former Miss Alabama, and Candace certainly had the look and demeanor of a Hollywood starlet from the fifties. Laurel claimed to be a nurse, and Yanny told us he was a surgeon. I saw the way Josh eyed Yanny's cutting skills when he attacked the beef Wellington after it was served. Either the knife was dull, or Yanny had zero finesse with one. Josh's raised brow said he hoped like hell Yanny was making up his profession, and if not, we wanted to make sure we'd never be laid out before him on an operating table.

"This is so tender you could cut it with a fork," Mitzi said, eyeing Yanny too.

"Thank you," Josh said.

Our table companions looked at him strangely. "Josh got to spend the day with Pierre making this delicious feast." I aimed a proud smile at my husband. "You did get the recipes, right?"

"Pierre will print them off for me before we head home. His creativity has gotten you to do something I never could."

There was only one food I refused to eat. I scrutinized my plate and saw zero signs of hateful fungi. I figured he was just giving me a hard time and continued eating.

"Is it your birthday or something?" Laurel asked.

"No," Josh said. "I just love to cook, so Gabe arranged it as a surprise for me."

"That's so sweet," Mitzi said, smiling her approval at me.

"It sounds like an apology or a bribe," Yanny said with a mouthful of food.

"Which is it? A thoughtful gift, an apology, or a bribe?" Candace asked.

I looked at Josh with a raised brow, encouraging him to field the question.

FIFTEEN

Josh

I KNEW WHAT THAT LOOK MEANT. IF I WANTED TO FAKE FIGHT with Gabe, then I'd have to be the one to throw the first fake punch. I could tell Gabe didn't see the necessity of a phony war between us, but I knew it would work best. By exposing our fake weaknesses, we had a much better chance at learning the real weaknesses of our enemies. In fact, I'd already seen it pan out when Clyde and Bonnie approached him earlier in the evening after our little tiff. Gabe wasn't afraid to challenge me or say what was on his mind, but he had a hard time working up fake angst and anger. He was a no-fuss kind of guy, and normally, I liked it.

"I think it's all of the above," I told Candace.

Yanny snorted but didn't look up from sawing through his meat. *Surgeon, my ass.* "I knew it. No one does genuinely nice things for people anymore." *Cynical much?*

His remark didn't make me angry; it made me sad for him. Gabe and I did nice things for each other all the damn time. This trip was a prime example of how thoughtful Gabe was, and I was ready to set Yanny straight. The sudden weight of Gabe's hand on my thigh calmed me down and reminded me this was nothing more than a game. I'd never see these people again, so did it matter what they thought of Gabe and Josh—the professor and his pole dancer?

"Mostly, he does nice things when he gets busy at the university and forgets important dates or the kids' activities *he* insisted they do so they're well-rounded." I did air quotes around the well-rounded bit, earning a smirk from the people around the table.

"Late nights at the university, huh, professor?" Yanny asked with a speculative look in his eye. "Let me guess," he said, leaning forward, "his teaching assistant is young, cute, and firm."

The hair stood up on the back of my neck, and my heart pinched painfully at the thought of another man earning Gabe's affection. Gabe's hand inched slowly up my thigh, assuring me he belonged to me and I to him. "And eager to please the professor," I added salaciously.

"And he thought this vacation would allow you to rekindle the fires you once had," Yanny said, nodding like he was a fucking relationship expert. He aimed a penetrating stare at Gabe and asked, "Has it worked, professor, or are you counting the days until you can return to your paramour?"

Paramour? Who said those things anymore? Gabe stiffened beside me and dug his fingers into my thigh. I worried he might throw his steak knife into Yanny's chest or bounce his crystal water glass off his smug face.

"We may have our problems, but Gabe would never cheat on me. He loves me, our children, and the life we've built together."

"He looked awfully chummy with dear old Henry earlier today."

I turned and looked at Gabe with a raised brow. My reaction was only partially fake since this was news to me. He told me he'd stayed up in our room all day reading which implied lack of interaction with other persons. How exactly did the little pow-wow go down, anyway?

"It was nothing," Gabe said. I felt his body tense, and his eyes widened with what was supposed to look like innocence; both things, combined with his tone of voice, screamed defensive mannerisms to me. Did he forget about my original major, and how much I loved studying humanity? What the hell did he have to feel defensive over?

"Stop creating trouble," Candace spoke up. "I also happened to be dining while Gabe passed through. Henry called him over to the table where he sat alone, and they spoke for two or three minutes tops. There was nothing flirty or inappropriate about the exchange."

I released a quiet sigh of relief. Gabe dug his fingers deeper into my thigh, letting me know he heard it. I knew he'd have something to say about my momentary doubt, and I'd offer a sincere apology because I had no defense for it. Jesus. This was Gabe, and he wore his honor like superheroes wore capes.

Mitzi tilted her head to the side and studied us unnervingly. "I got the impression Henry suggested what you could do with your free time."

"See," Yanny said. "I wasn't the only one who saw the exchange accurately. Miss Disney Princess only sees what she wants to."

Candace's face turned bright red with fury. "Disney Princess?" Okay, it was hard to take her seriously with that voice. Could she surprise us like the lady in the *Police Academy* movies Gabe loves so much? Possibly. It sure looked like she was working up to it. "I'll have you know—" Mitzi covered Candace's hand where it rested on the table, cutting off whatever she was about to say. I knew it would have been huge. I bet Candace's demeanor was all an act. She was probably an engineer or something really brainy. I had the distinct feeling she wasn't happy about her role and was about to set Yanny straight and ruin her cover.

Yanny must've sensed it too because he raised his glass and silently toasted her. Then he turned his laser-like gaze on Gabe, and I knew I wasn't going to like the words he spoke next. "Did he, or did he not, slip you a piece of paper?" I didn't just dislike the words; I *hated* them.

Candace leaned across the table and looked at me. I couldn't look away from her direct, no-nonsense expression. "He gave it right back. I don't even think he looked at it."

I looked at Gabe. "Is that true?"

"We'll discuss this privately," Gabe said stiffly, but the gentle motion of his hand on my leg assured me his words were part of his act.

"Teach, you should've never allowed yourself to fall in love with your private dancer let alone marry him. He's never going to understand guys like us."

"Excuse me?" Gabe asked. I must say, his arrogant tone of voice was doing delicious things to my body. "You don't know enough about me to make a bold statement like that." Oh, how he bristled gloriously. Damn, I wanted to role play the naughty professor and his slutty personal assistant when we got back to our room. "You know nothing of our life to base an opinion on."

"According to your husband, your attention is roaming."

"He isn't there to see if my 'attention is roaming.' Josh is projecting his insecurities onto me. He's the one who thinks he's not good enough for me, not the other way around. I am proud of him and the life we have together. All marriages have dry spells and hurdles to jump."

"Especially with juggling kids," I said, turning to look at Gabe. "We need to work harder on making time for us." I leaned in for a quick kiss while Gabe took advantage of my shift to cup my crotch beneath the table. I didn't know it was possible for me to have anything left in the tank, but my engine wanted to fire to life.

"Aww," Laurel said, covering her heart. "My faith is renewed." *So much for making the other competitors think we had marital problems.*

Yanny snorted while Mitzi and Candace smiled endearingly. We spent the rest of the dinner discussing less controversial topics, but I noticed how Yanny diverted the conversation anytime we steered too close to his work by saying things like, "No shop talk while on vacation."

"Not even to tell us about your specialty?" Mitzi asked innocently. I noticed she kept watching his hands too. I wouldn't let Yanny cut coupons, let alone my flesh.

"Yanny, stop being so modest. He's one of the top cardiothoracic surgeons in our state."

"Country," Yanny corrected. The douche didn't want to talk shop, but he sure as hell wanted to brag about his fake accomplishments.

"Oh! It's good to know we'll be in good hands if we have an accident and break a bone or something."

Laurel's eyes widened slightly, and I could tell she was worried Yanny would blow their cover. "No, dear," she said patiently. "A cardiothoracic surgeon performs surgery on the thorax region which is your heart and lungs. We don't want to be in need of his services this weekend."

"Oh," Candace said wide-eyed. "Definitely not."

Gabe rubbed his hands together gleefully when the waiter delivered our desserts to our table. Then he lowered his head and inhaled deeply. "Boozy pie," he said lustily.

"I was so excited when Chef Pierre announced what we were making for dessert. He used the top-notch bourbon too."

"Bourbon? In a pie?" Mitzi asked. "I've never heard of such a thing."

I turned my attention to her. "It's my recipe and only the best apple pie you will ever eat."

"We'll just see about that," Mitzi said, forking a tiny bite in her mouth. Her eyes widened when the flavor burst on her tongue. "Oh, my!"

"I know," I replied cockily. "Dig in, everyone." I wanted all the adoration and wouldn't bother to deny it. I glanced over to see if the other tables had started in on their desserts and noticed the tables were empty.

"I want their pie," Gabe said. "They don't get a redo."

"I didn't even know they'd left," I confessed.

Gabe leaned over and pressed his mouth to my ear. "You were either too busy getting pissed when you thought I was flirting with Henry, or you were fantasizing about playing naughty professor when we get back to our room." Gabe leaned back and raised a brow, daring me to deny it.

"Guilty," I whispered back but didn't tell him I'd thought of both of those things. I'd wait and spring it on him when we were alone.

"Brenda Leigh would've noticed." Gabe winked playfully and went back to eating.

He was right though. I should've been aware that six people left the room, especially the two hostile groups. Where did they go? Back to their rooms to cool things down or heat them up? Did I even want to know? *Hell yes.*

"Oh darn," Juliette said when she entered the dining area. "I hoped they would reconsider their decision to avoid group activities. I mean, solving the murder mystery will involve interaction between everyone." She shook her head sadly. "At least there are the six of you to play along."

"I think we've gotten to know each other well enough over dinner," Gabe said. He went around the table rattling off the things he knew about everyone to demonstrate. "We've talked plenty."

"Don't sound so stodgy, dear," I teased. "It won't hurt us to spend a bit more time together before the festivities begin. Besides, it would seem the other three couples have an advantage over us since they know each other so well."

"Excellent point," Juliette said, beaming her approval at me. "Just one group activity."

There was a mixture of grumbled acceptance and exuberant replies, but we agreed to move over to the bar while they set up a table of activities. Gabe drank scotch on the rocks while I ordered one of my typical fruity concoctions. I noticed that all the couples seemed to wander off to give themselves a bit of space. There was a heated exchange between Yanny and Laurel while Mitzi looked to be coaching Candace. I suspected she was reminding her to play dumb. As for me, I played the adoring husband role so very well. I couldn't wait to get back to our room to demonstrate my adoration.

"You make me feel like I'm twenty again," Gabe whispered in my ear.

"Yeah, but it would make me like twelve."

"That's so gross. You damn well know what I mean."

"You might have to get the paddle out and punish me," I told Gabe.

"Did you pack a paddle?" He sounded excited about the idea.

"You'll have to wait and find out."

"We're going to get this socializing crap over with soon so we can get upstairs and—"

"Trying to store up as many sexy times for when you return to your tired, dusty old marital bed?" Yanny asked snidely.

I scowled at him while laughing on the inside. There was nothing old, tired, or dusty about our sex life. "Something like that," I mumbled.

"Let's get started," Juliette said. "Feel free to wander around the room until you find an activity table to your liking."

There were a variety of things to choose from Twenty Questions to Never Have I Ever, but the one we all seemed to navigate toward was the one with popular social media memes. One asked you to quote a popular line from a movie or song from the year you were born so the rest of the group could guess. Everyone easily guessed until it was Mitzi's turn.

"Of all the gin joints in all the towns in all the world, she walks into mine," Mitzi said. "Candace isn't allowed to guess since she knows the answer."

"*Gone with the Wind*," Laurel guessed.

"That was 1939," Mitzi said. "Close."

"*Wizard of Oz*," Yanny guessed. Did he really think there were gin joints in Oz?

"Also 1939," Mitzi said.

"*Woman of the Year*," Gabe suggested. "It is one of my mom's favorites. I think it was from the forties."

"Same year, wrong movie," Mitzi told him, smiling fondly. She sure didn't look like a seventy-six-year-old woman.

"*Casablanca*," I casually said.

"Did you guess, or did you know?" Mitzi asked.

"I knew. I've seen the movie hundreds of times. I think it's time to watch it again."

The next printed meme in the pile wasn't as fun, and the third was just silly, but the last one created quite a stir. It had a picture of a jail cell and listed all kinds of sexual activities with the number of years you'd get in jail for each "crime." You tallied up the numbers next to each one to see how many years total you'd spend in jail.

"Oh my," Candace said breathily when she looked over the list.

"I'm frightfully boring. I only get like three years in jail."

"Three?" Yanny asked, sounding appalled. "Sweetheart, I will happily help you scratch some items off this list."

"Hey, asshole," I said. "It's a social media meme, not her bucket list."

"No need to get so hostile," Yanny replied, sitting back in his chair. "Afraid you won't measure up to me?"

"What's your number?"

Yanny cracked a joke about needing a calculator and made a big production of adding the numbers up on his cell phone. "Sixty-nine!" he boasted. "What a fitting number. Your turn. I know you think you have the advantage over me since I've never had anal sex or fucked someone of the same sex, but I doubt it."

"Eighty-two," I said without having to add. "I just answered this last week."

"Eighty-two?" Gabe asked. "Wow."

"Why are you looking all shocked, professor? Most of these numbers I've racked up with you, and I do believe your number is higher once you add yours up."

"No way," Gabe said, taking the printout. "I… Oh, yeah. I have done most of these things. Which one have I done that you haven't?"

"At least two," I told him. "I've never had sex with an ex after we broke up nor have I had sex with a friend. I believe you've done both."

"It's the same guy, so only one counts," Gabe replied. He had me there. "Okay, my number is eighty-five."

Laurel blushed when she tallied up her number. "Fifty-eight. It's a pretty respectable number."

Mitzi went last. "I don't need to add it up to know I beat you all since there isn't one thing on the list I haven't done."

"Mom!" Candace exclaimed in horror. I could tell she wanted to ask questions.

Mitzi just shook her head. "Don't ask if you can't handle the truth."

"I think it's time to call it a night. Clearly, my mother is overtired."

"I am not overtired. I am fully capable of recognizing all the delicious things I've gotten up to throughout my adult years." A wistful gleam shone in the older woman's light blue eyes. "Those were the days."

"Hey there, firecracker," Yanny said lecherously. "You're not dead yet, and the night is still young."

"We're going," Gabe said, scooting his chair back suddenly and rising to his feet. "Goodnight, everyone." He turned and left the room at a brisk walk. I rose just as quickly and bid them all a good evening before I followed. I caught him right before he reached the staircases.

"You played Professor Prude really good there at the end. I nearly blew it by making you out to be a sex fiend."

Gabe chuckled. "Some of those answers were so common that everyone should have included them. I mean, who hasn't used sex as a form of bartering?"

"And what exactly do you use your dick to barter for, Gabe?"

"An extra half hour of sleep and the sports package on cable to name a few."

"That's it?" I asked, stopping at our suite door so he could unlock it.

"What do you use sex to barter for?" Gabe asked.

"If I tell you, it will no longer be effective."

"You little impertinent brat," Gabe said, sounding sexy and commanding. Naughty professor indeed.

"What did the note say?" I asked, changing the subject suddenly.

Gabe cupped my face with both hands and looked me square in the eyes. "I didn't read it. I wasn't interested in anything he had to say or offer. You're it for me, Sunshine."

"What did he say before slipping the note to you?"

"He talked about the storm the newscasters predicted would hit tonight and asked if I recommended anything off the lunch menu. That was the gist of our conversation."

"Okay."

"Okay?" Gabe sounded skeptical.

"I trust you."

"So, you didn't doubt me for even a second?" I thought back to the conversation at dinner. I didn't like how Gabe had left parts out, but I didn't believe he did it to hurt me.

"Half a second maybe, but then I remembered I married an honorable man who freaking adores me."

"How are we supposed to have fake makeup sex if we don't get into a fake fight?"

"We'll have naughty-professor sex instead. Take everything off, but put the jacket back on. Oh, and I want you to keep that pipe in your mouth the entire time I give you head. If the pipe falls out, then I stop."

"I like this game."

I hid my smirk from Gabe's face because I doubted he could keep the pipe clamped between his teeth while I worked my mouth up and down his hard length. The only noises my man made were grunts of pleasure, and he somehow managed to hold onto the pipe until the last drop of cum slid down my throat. Gabe turned me over his knee and pretended to punish his wayward assistant with firm slaps to my ass followed by the most delicious hand job ever.

Sometime in the middle of the night, a hellacious bolt of lightning lit the room followed by a roll of thunder so loud it shook the inn. It startled me awake.

"Here comes the storm," Gabe mumbled. "Juliette said there are emergency flashlights, candles, and matches in the bedside table drawers. I guess losing power is a pretty common occurrence."

It was the most frightening storm I'd ever witnessed in my life. The lightning was so intense it made me flinch, and the roaring thunder made me nestle tighter against Gabe. There was no way in hell I could sleep through a severe storm of that magnitude, so I just held onto him for dear life and prayed it would end soon. The electricity did go out which made it more uncomfortable in our room without the air-conditioning and ceiling fan circulating above us.

"Don't even think about it," I said to Gabe as he tried to shimmy away from my body heat.

"I was just going to open the balcony doors to let some fresh air in."

"Okay, but come right back."

Gabe stopped and headed back to the bed long before he reached the balcony doors. "The rain is too strong and blowing in this direction."

"Damn."

Gabe returned to our bed and kicked the blankets to our feet before pulling me into his arms. It took forever for the storm to wind down and move past us. "Now we can get some fresh air," my husband said.

Gabe climbed out of bed and opened the balcony doors. The breeze felt incredible, and it carried harmonious, singing voices into our room. I sat up quickly, prepared to go out on the balcony so I could hear them better, but a blood-curdling scream sliced through the serene moment.

I reached for my phone on the bedside table to see what time it was. "Surely they're not starting the murder mystery at five after two in the morning."

"I don't think the scream was part of an act, Sunshine," Gabe said, walking quickly to his discarded clothes on the floor.

"All of these people are probably paid actors," I grumbled as I got dressed too. "There better be a real dead body down there and some seriously strong coffee."

"Damn," Gabe said. "I don't have any cell phone service."

I looked at my phone and saw "no service" in the upper left corner. "Me either."

"I bet the landlines are down too."

We grabbed the flashlights from the bedside table and headed out into the hallway at the same time as everyone else who looked as exhausted and shocked as we felt. The only two people missing were Petal and Georgia. Another scream rang out into the night, making most of us jump in alarm.

"Damn that woman," George said, looking and sounding none too concerned. "What's wrong? Did they cut Georgia off at the bar?"

I didn't care what George said. Her anguish wasn't a result of being denied a drink. If Georgia was accounted for, then where was Petal?

SIXTEEN

Gabe

"Where's Brittany...I mean Petal?" Henry abruptly asked as if he'd just taken a headcount and realized his lover was missing.

"Everyone go back to your rooms," I said firmly. "I'll go down and help Georgia. Do not come down these stairs unless I tell you to."

"I'm coming with you," Henry said. "She's my—"

"I need you to stay here, Henry."

"I'll stay with him," Josh said, stepping up beside Henry and placing a comforting hand on his shoulder. "Go on downstairs, Gabe. We'll be fine."

I aimed my flashlight in front of me and jogged down the stairs. I could hear muffled conversation up above but couldn't make out what they were saying over the pounding of my heart. I was just glad they were listening.

"Help! Somebody help her!" Georgia wailed pitifully from somewhere on the main floor. "No. No. No. No. No," she kept saying over and over again. Following the sound of her anguished voice, I had a strong suspicion help would arrive too late for Petal, aka Brittany. I also wished I had my gun with me.

Georgia's grief-stricken voice was joined by two others I recognized. When I entered what appeared to be a library, Georgia was kneeling in the center of the room with Geneva and Juliette on either side of her. It appeared that the women were trying to console her. They either hastily set their flashlights on the floor or dropped them because the three beams of light were aimed in opposite directions.

"We need to call the police," Geneva said to Juliette over Georgia's head.

"Landlines are down," Juliette replied. "I can't get cell service either."

"Neither can I," I added. All three women jumped to their feet and screamed in fright.

"Whoa," I said calmly, aiming the flashlight away from their frightened faces so I wouldn't blind them. "It's me, Gabe."

"Go back upstairs," Geneva said. "You don't need to see this."

"Geneva, I'm not a professor; I'm the police captain for the Blissville Police Department. What's happened?"

Juliette picked up the flashlights and handed one to Geneva before guiding a sobbing Georgia over to the sofa. Once they moved away, I got my first look at Brittany. Her blue eyes and painted mouth both registered the shock and horror she'd felt in her final moments. Her still, petite body was draped in a silvery silk gown marred with blood from stab wounds caused by the knife lying on the floor beside her in a pool of blood. I counted five bloody gashes in her gown. I wouldn't know if there were more on her back unless I rolled her over which I was not authorized to do.

"Have any of you touched the body?" I asked.

Geneva shook her head. "Juliette and I just arrived seconds before you did. We heard the screaming in our room and came to see what happened."

"Geneva, will you go to the kitchen and see if you can find a pair of latex gloves for me?" I'd seen plenty of chefs wear gloves similar to those I wore at crime scenes. I hoped Pierre kept a stash in his kitchen. "Are there any other employees on site we can send for help? We need to get the sheriff's department here as soon as possible." I could estimate the time of death based on the stage of rigor mortis, but the coroner would be able to determine a more exact window of time.

"Sure, Gabe," Geneva said, sounding relieved to have something helpful to do. Some people responded well in a crisis, and it appeared both Geneva and Juliette had the gift. "I'll be right back."

Until she came back with the gloves, I stayed away from the body. I shined my flashlight around the room looking for signs of a struggle or evidence left behind. I noticed a set of French doors were hanging wide open and the wood floor in front of them was wet.

I cautiously approached in my bare feet, hoping to see if there were footprints in the moisture on the floor I could at least photograph, but there were none. There were no other obvious clues I could see in the dark. None of the books or knickknacks on the shelf appeared disturbed, and none of the furniture was knocked over to indicate a struggle had ensued.

I quickly made my way over to Georgia and knelt in front of her. "Georgia, I know you've suffered a terrible shock, but I need you to tell me what brought you downstairs and everything you saw when you entered this room."

Georgia rubbed her face to wipe the tears, but they kept coming. I wanted to tell her to take her time, but we had a killer among us. I whispered encouraging words to her, hoping it would help calm her down a bit. She tried talking to me but only sobs escaped every time she opened her mouth.

"Here, Gabe," Geneva said, rushing back into the room. "Will these gloves work?"

"Yes, ma'am. Thank you."

"Is there anything else I can do to help?"

"I need you to guard the door like your son guarded the basket during his career. No one else comes in here until the sheriff arrives. After I'm done talking to Georgia, I will send her up to her room."

"Should I go talk to the others? Surely they've heard the commotion and realize something tragic has happened."

Josh. One of the people upstairs with him could be the killer. I wanted—needed—to see for myself he was safe, but I trusted him to be smart and take care of himself. I couldn't leave the body unattended until help arrived.

"You can tell them there's been an accident and they need to stay in their rooms until they're told otherwise. And, Geneva, is there anyone here who can leave to go get the sheriff?" I asked. "Another employee who lives on site perhaps?"

"We have several employees who live in the converted carriage house. I have no way of calling them with the phones down."

"I can get dressed and drive to the sheriff's department," Juliette said. "Geneva and I are the only ones who have easy access to cars because everyone else's, including the guests, are parked in the lot behind the barns."

"Honey, you be careful," Geneva said. "You'll be driving toward the wicked storm that just passed through."

"I'll be fine," Juliette said, rising from the couch. She crossed to Geneva and embraced her tight. "I'll be back with help as soon as I can."

The exchange between the two women seemed to take Georgia's mind off her tragedy long enough for me to position myself in front of her so she couldn't see Petal's body.

"Let's try this again," I said softly. Georgia tried to lean around and look behind me, but I stopped her by gently placing my hands on her biceps. "Look at me, Georgia. Petal is gone, so we need to focus our energy on finding out who killed her."

Georgia focused her eyes on me. "Brittany," she said softly. "Her name is—" Her words broke off on a choked sob. "Her name was Brittany Blake."

"Georgia, tell me everything you remember, starting with what time you went upstairs, why you went up early, and what happened afterward."

She told me they had no interest in playing silly games and getting to know anyone. She thought it was half past eight when they went upstairs to their rooms. "We were all getting along so well if you know what I mean." I nodded for her to continue. "I had battled a nasty headache all day, and I don't sleep very well away from home. I took a sleeping pill at around ten o'clock. Brittany was lying in bed with me while the men played poker in the other room."

"How do you know what time it was?" I asked.

"Channel Four news was on, and their broadcast is always an hour earlier than the other local stations," Georgia replied. "I woke up at some point during the storm. I noticed George was sleeping soundly beside me instead of Brittany. When I looked in her room, only Henry was in their bed."

"What made you go to her room?" I asked. I thought it was kind of strange.

"I wanted to make sure she was okay because she's terrified of storms. She can't sleep through them and tremors like a Chihuahua.

Brittany likes to distract herself with television, but I quickly realized the power was out, so I thought she might've wandered down here to the library to get a book to read."

"Do you recall if the French doors were already open when you came in?" I suspected they were since there were no signs of footprints in the water droplets on the floor.

"I did notice they were open because I saw the faint flashes of lightning from the storm that moved past and I saw Brittany's body lying in the shaft of moonlight coming through them. I-I saw all the blood and the knife beside her and screamed."

"You didn't hear any other sounds in the house when you came downstairs? No movement anywhere?"

"None," Georgia said then sniffled. "Who would want to do this to her?"

A certain brother and sister duo came to mind, but I shoved the thoughts aside. I could worry about interviewing suspects later. *Wait.* This wasn't my jurisdiction. My responsibility was to secure the crime scene and make sure no one left. Whichever deputy arrived on the scene would handle the interviews. I would state the facts as I knew them and not interfere with their investigation.

"Georgia, why don't you go upstairs and be with your husband and friend right now."

"Do I tell them what happened to Brittany?"

"It's not possible to keep it a secret, and they'd rather hear it from you than a virtual stranger. Please don't share any details about how she died and ask them to stay upstairs until law enforcement arrives."

Georgia appeared to have aged at least fifteen years since the last time I saw her, but it happens when you stumble across your murdered lover slash friend in the middle of the night. She was wobbly on her feet when I helped her stand, and I was concerned she would hurt herself trying to get back upstairs.

"Let me help you, Miss Georgia," Geneva said, reentering the room. "Henry is sitting with Josh right now. He knows something is wrong, but I was afraid to say too much."

"Thank you, Geneva," Georgia weakly replied.

After the ladies left, I returned to the body in the middle of the room. I was careful to avoid the pool of blood when I knelt by the body and slipped on the gloves Geneva brought me. I was glad I'd stuck my phone in my rear pocket out of habit because I was able to take pictures for evidence. I set the flashlight on the floor beside me, aiming it at the body, and picked up Brittany's right hand. I noticed three things: her wrists were loose, so rigor mortis hadn't started yet, there were no signs of defensive wounds, and there didn't appear to be signs of foreign fibers or DNA from her assailant. I photographed her right hand to show those things then moved around to do the same with her left hand. Whoever attacked Brittany caught her by complete surprise, and it was within the last three hours. Rigor set in after three hours and lasted up to thirty-six hours. I checked the time on my phone. The time of death occurred sometime after eleven thirty.

Stabbing deaths were almost always personal, and I doubted this homicide was an exception, especially after the animosity I witnessed this week. I turned my attention to the knife itself but didn't touch it. I recognized it as a brand Josh drooled over but refused to buy. I couldn't understand why until I googled them and saw the price. Only professional chefs or extremely wealthy people would drop more than a thousand dollars for a set of knives. This wasn't the kind of knife you packed around with you to kill someone; it was the kind you grabbed because it was handy.

I photographed the knife so we...*they*...could verify it came out of Tarlington House's kitchen. An agonized male scream echoed through the house followed by the pounding of feet on the stairs. There was nothing else I could do in the library in the dark, so I quickly ran to the library door just in time to prevent Henry from entering the room.

"Let me see her," he shouted. "I need to see her. Brittany!"

I muscled him out of the doorway and shut the door closed behind me, blocking her prone body from his view. "Henry, you do not want to go in there right now."

"Yes, I do. Get out of my way."

He tried to wrestle past me, but I was able to get him in a hold until he stopped fighting me. "Calm down, Henry. I can't let you go in there. I don't want you to see her like that, and I need to keep the scene as clean as possible for the cops."

Henry went from trying to resist to clinging to me. "She can't be gone. I won't believe it."

"Go back upstairs, Henry. George and Georgia need you, and you need them too." I couldn't begin to understand the relationship they all shared, but it was obvious there was genuine affection between the two couples. "Avoid talking to the other couples; the last thing an investigation needs is for all of you to start comparing stories and mixing up facts. I would pack a few essential items because there is absolutely no way they're going to allow us to stay on site while they investigate a homicide."

"She's gone?"

"I'm terribly sorry, but she is."

Henry nodded slowly then turned and went back upstairs, leaving just Geneva and me downstairs.

Once it was quiet, Geneva started to shake. "I can't believe this has happened, Gabe."

I put my arm around the older woman and hugged her. "I'm so sorry, Geneva. I know it's a terrible shock. Would you mind going upstairs to sit with my husband?"

"Of course."

I hoped like hell it wouldn't take long for the cavalry to arrive, but it took three hours. There were downed trees on county roads which delayed Juliette getting to the sheriff's department. I identified myself to Detectives Holbrook and Bernard from the sheriff's department when they arrived and showed them my business card. My badge was locked in the glove box of the minivan, but they assured me they didn't need it. Luckily, the power and phone services were restored not long after they arrived. They were chilly toward me at first but warmed up after a quick call to the Blissville PD confirmed that I was indeed one of the boys in blue. It didn't matter to them that I was from a different state or that I was a small-town cop instead of a deputy sheriff; we wanted the same thing—to catch Brittany's killer. Had I been a federal cop, they might not have been as friendly.

I recalled for them the events from my perspective and emailed them the crime scene photos before permanently deleting them from my phone. As I suspected, we were permitted to pack a few essentials, and our bags were searched before they loaded us into a van and took us to the sheriff's department to conduct interviews. Afterward, we would be permitted to stay at the nearest hotel until we were allowed to leave the area.

I was just happy to know my husband was safe and away from danger. I planned to use my influence to ensure he stayed that way.

SEVENTEEN

Josh

"HOW ARE YOU TODAY, MR. ROMAN-WYATT?" DETECTIVE HOLDEN asked me. I cocked a brow in response. "It's a silly question, I know. It just tends to break the ice."

"Honestly, Detectives, this entire situation is surreal. Gabe brought me here for a murder mystery weekend, but I guarantee this wasn't what he wanted." Both of the men snickered. "I'm never letting him make vacation plans for us ever again. I will inform him of this as soon as I'm allowed to see him." We were separated and watched like hawks when we arrived at the sheriff's department. I understood why, but I didn't have to like it.

"Tell me what you can about Brittany 'Petal' Blake," Detective Bernard said.

"I know next to nothing about the real person," I replied. "I can only tell you about the facets she showed me in the brief time I was around her."

When Gabe came upstairs after the detectives and coroner arrived, he had instructed me only to answer what I knew. He told me embellishing could hinder the investigation. I believe he compared it to adding fancy fruit and crap to a perfectly good cocktail. *What the fuck did a garnish have to do with a murder investigation?* Anyway, I nodded and paid attention because this was his area of expertise. It wasn't like he came into the salon and told me how to color someone's hair. Gabe said I could share impressions with the detectives because those can be very helpful, but I needed to make it clear they were my thoughts and not facts.

"Fair enough," Detective Holden said. "Tell me about your interactions with the deceased."

I had no idea if they'd already interviewed Gabe, and I knew it didn't matter if they had. I needed to repeat every single thing I remembered. I bet they didn't expect me to divulge as much as I did. The style of her gown or the way she styled her hair probably weren't relevant to the murder investigation, but I told them anyway. Their eyes widened when I got to the part where I discovered the two couples were either swingers or were two halves of a bigger whole. Both detectives refrained from commenting about anything salacious and just maintained professional demeanors as they walked me through my interactions with the deceased and everyone else staying at the inn. Detective Holden seemed happy to allow Detective Bernard to take all the notes while he kept his hawk-like eyes trained on me. I didn't squirm or wiggle beneath his intense gaze because I had nothing to hide.

"What was said in the group before Gabe went downstairs to investigate?" Detective Bernard asked. I figured he was asking everyone to see if any of us picked up on anything unusual.

"George joked about his wife yelling because the bar was closed or something silly, but it wasn't that kind of scream. We all seemed to realize who else was missing at the same time." I shivered as I recalled the tormented, heart-breaking sounds Georgia made when she found Brittany's body.

"William 'Henry' Blake went to your room with you instead of returning to his room?" Detective Bernard asked.

"Yes," I said, nodding. "He was extremely distraught and wanted to follow Gabe downstairs. I promised Gabe I would stay with Henry to try and keep him calm and out of the way. I didn't get the impression George would be very helpful."

"Did anyone else leave an impression on you?" Detective Holden asked. "Any comments or reactions that seemed out of place."

"No villainous laughs," I told them. "Everyone genuinely seemed shell-shocked."

"Except for Dylan Howard, who you know as George," Detective Bernard said, looking at his notes. "Would you say he seemed more annoyed about having his sleep interrupted than concerned about why his wife was screaming?"

"It was the impression he gave me," I replied honestly.

Detective Holden's eyebrows lowered slightly like he was working out a problem, but his expression quickly returned to a neutral mask. "What did William Blake, or Henry, say once he was inside your suite?"

"Mostly it was incoherent mumbling as he rocked back and forth on the sofa beside me. He'd covered his face with his hands and alternated saying 'she's okay; she's fine' and 'this can't be happening' until Geneva came upstairs to tell us Brittany had died."

Detective Bernard sat up straighter in his chair. "Geneva

Louderback only said Brittany had died? She didn't say she was killed?"

"That's right. She didn't tell us Brittany was killed, and she didn't say where her body was found. She only said that Brittany had died and Gabe needed us to stay inside while we waited for law enforcement to arrive."

"William Blake stayed with you this entire time, Mr. Roman-Wyatt," Detective Holden asked.

"When he first heard the news, he leaped to his feet and bolted from the room. Geneva followed after him. I could hear him shouting, and Gabe trying to calm him down. It sounded like they got into a scuffle—"

"A fight?" Detective Bernard asked to clarify.

"No, not a fist fight or anything. It sounded like Gabe was blocking him from going inside the room. We were too far away to hear the exact words spoken, but I got the impression Gabe was trying to protect him and the scene. He wouldn't want William to see Brittany in that condition. I think Gabe subdued him so he couldn't enter the library. It wasn't long before Geneva brought him back upstairs to me."

"Did William say anything?"

"No. He just curled into the corner of the couch and sobbed. He was truly inconsolable."

"Have you ever been inside the library at Tarlington House?" Detective Holden asked me.

"No, sir." I told him about the rooms I had visited inside the inn and the locations on the property even though it probably wasn't relevant. Of course, I left off the sex part when I mentioned watching the sunrise from the lighthouse. It wasn't relevant. "We'd been told a library was located on the first floor and where we could find it, but I'd brought my own books to read."

"What about your husband? Are you aware of him visiting the library?" Detective Bernard asked.

"I am not, but we were apart for several hours yesterday while I helped prepare the special dinner. Gabe didn't mention entering the library to me. In fact, he wouldn't even tell me where the body was found, so this is the first I heard about it."

"So, we won't find your fingerprints in the library or any personal property belonging to you?" Detective Holden asked as a follow-up.

"No, sirs."

"We've heard about the deceased getting into an argument and a fight with a Miss Beatrice Danner. I believe you would know her as Bonnie," Bernard said.

"I was engaged in a different conversation when the altercation broke out, but Henry and I rushed to break them up when they were rolling around on the floor. I mean, William and I." The fake names turned out to be a huge annoyance, and I imagined the detectives were having a blast keeping it all straight.

"It is your belief the women were fighting over William Blake?"

"It's the impression I got from talking to Gabe after we were sent to our rooms without dinner," I told Detective Bernard, earning a chuckle.

The interview wound down after that because I didn't have much else to share with them. Gabe and I had embarked on a sexfest mission and had only planned to surface for the murder mystery. We had ourselves a murder mystery all right. I was left alone again in the small, windowless room to wait until it was time to go to the hotel. I was hungry, exhausted, and missed my husband like crazy. I folded my arms on the table and rested my head against my forearms. There was no way in hell I'd be able to sleep under the circumstances, but it felt good just to close my eyes and rest. I looked up when the door opened a few minutes later, expecting to see one or both detectives returning to ask more questions.

"Hey, Sunshine," Gabe said softly, looking as exhausted as I felt. He placed a sack of food and a drink carrier with two large cups on the table. "I thought you might be hungry."

I rose to my feet and walked into his open arms. "I'm so happy to see you. Are you okay?" I didn't think it was possible ever to get used to seeing dead bodies, especially victims of a violent crime. I didn't know how Brittany died, but it was obvious it wasn't from natural causes.

"I'll be better once we're cleared to leave." Gabe released me and pulled out a chair at the table. "In the meantime, we might as well have a bite to eat."

I don't know who was responsible for the thick deli sandwiches, chips, and drinks, but I was grateful. "How long do you think it will be before they transport us to the hotel?"

"I have no idea since I'm not in the loop."

"You're not getting treated like a suspect, are you? You're a police captain for fuck's sake. I thought you boys in blue stuck together."

"I'm getting treated with the respect they'd show every officer while they work through an investigation, but no, I don't feel like they suspect me of foul play. The fact that I'm sitting in here with you right now is evidence of their respect. None of the other couples are eating lunch together."

"Yeah, because they're all suspicious as fuck, Gabe. Neither of us had reason to want Brittany dead."

"I'm hoping we can leave tomorrow."

"Tomorrow?" I asked. "They'll keep us at the station all night? I thought they were bussing us over to the hotel."

"They can keep us here as long as the law allows, but I think they're planning on transporting us to the hotel fairly soon."

"Then what did you mean about leaving tomorrow?"

"I meant that I'm getting our rental van from the inn and driving us home as soon as they give me the okay."

"You're leaving an active investigation?"

"It's not *my* investigation, Sunshine. I'm not the police captain in this scenario; I'm your husband. I need to get you away from danger and home to our children where you'll be safe," Gabe said, pinning me with an intense look that said it wasn't something he was willing to debate either. "Holden and Bernard have this under control. The South Carolina Law Enforcement Division will send them help if they need it. There's no reason for me to stay."

"You don't care about what happens?" I asked appalled. "Gabe, we dined and had conversations with her. How can you not care?"

Gabe calmly set his sandwich down on the wrapper and wiped his mouth. "Of course I care someone drove a fucking butcher knife into the body of a twenty-eight-year-old woman, Josh. I am appalled her life could be snuffed out so quickly and coldly. I'm more terrified you and I might've sat across from the sick fuck who killed her. Do you have any idea how hard it was for me to protect the crime scene downstairs when all I wanted to do was be with you? Have you any idea the scenarios that flitted through my mind? Yes, I am a police captain sworn to uphold the law, but I also took an oath to love, cherish, and protect you too. I've done my part to uphold the law, and now, I want to take my husband home."

It was really hard to argue with his logic when he looked at me with so much love and conviction even though I wanted to give it my best shot. "Fine," I replied. "We'll leave as soon as we get the green light."

"We're driving straight home. I'm only stopping for gas, and we can use those opportunities to stretch. All food items will be purchased through a drive-thru or at the gas station."

"What about Bonita?" I asked. "She's hoping we'll stop by on our way back through Tennessee."

"Josh, I have no idea when they'll let us go home, and I'm sure Bonita wouldn't appreciate us showing up at her doorstep at some random hour in the middle of the night. I will call and explain to her as best I can. I mean it, Josh. We're going straight home with no detours."

"I will agree to your terms under one condition."

"Let's hear it?"

"You are never *ever* going to plan another vacation trip."

Gabe smiled at me for the first time since all hell broke loose. "You've got yourself a deal."

EIGHTEEN

Gabe

"I don't think I've ever been so excited to lie down in bedbug-infested sheets in all my life," Josh said with disdain, scanning the hotel room the sheriff's department procured for us after they wrapped up the interviews. "You'd think your police captain status would've garnered better accommodations." He dropped his bag on the ground and flopped onto the bed which was a testimony to just how tired he was after staying at the station until nearly 5 p.m.

"My police captain status earned us a 'free to go home' card, snark ass," I informed him. He jerked to a sitting position and looked at me with accusing eyes. He looked as if not telling him we didn't have to stay at the hotel was a bigger betrayal than not telling him about Henry's flirting and note passing. "I'm too fucking tired to make the drive tonight."

Josh flopped back down dramatically. "Not that we have transportation beyond the sheriff's van. I doubt their generosity extends to letting us borrow it."

"Holden and Bernard are retrieving the minivan keys from the valet cabinet and bringing it to us. They should be here soon. Rumor has it Holden will also bring us some of his wife's home cooking. We'll be set for the night and can head home in the morning."

"Having second thoughts about leaving?" Josh asked.

I was horribly conflicted about choosing the right thing to do. Walking away from a homicide investigation was against my nature, but it wasn't *my* investigation. Holden and Bernard were excellent detectives, and they'd leave no stone unturned. I was confident they'd catch the killer. Josh's safety had to come first. I thought about putting him on a plane and sending him home without me, but it didn't feel right either. Holden and Bernard said they'd stay in touch and keep me in the loop, so it would have to be enough.

"No," I replied.

"You're so bad at lying," Josh said. "You want to solve this case as badly as I do."

"Of course I want the case to get solved, but I don't have to be the one who does it. I'm not the control freak in this relationship." I sat on the twin bed across from his.

Josh snorted. "You're Captain Control Freak."

"I'm about to be Captain Cranky Pants if I don't get some food and a decent night's sleep."

"I think I could even skip the food in favor of sleeping."

I glanced up from reading the latest text from Adrian and saw he was on the verge of falling asleep. I knew I'd be right behind him if I lay down, and I wanted the minivan keys in my hand before that happened. I stayed in the upright position and bantered back and forth with Adrian. He was shocked and sorry to hear about the young lady who was killed at the inn, but it didn't stop him from cracking jokes.

Hey, maybe Lyric can hook you up with your own television show! Vacation Disasters!

I was thinking Deadliest Vacations. The viewers will expect to see me swimming with sharks, but instead, I'll be staying in remote inns with swingers, liars, and killers.

Good one, Gabe. You let me know if there's anything you need at all. I know you want to solve the crime so bad it hurts, but get the hell out of there and let Holden and Bernard do their jobs.

We'll be home sometime tomorrow. I'll keep you posted.

You better, partner.

A knock vibrated the hotel door, rousing Josh from his dozed state. "Who's here?" He hadn't been asleep long, but he looked like he was really out of it.

"I'm sure it's only Bernard and Holden." I checked the peephole, and Bernard stood on the other side doing a cute finger wave until Holden shoved him out of the way to hold up the bag of food he carried. The door was so damn flimsy I could smell the fried chicken through it.

"That'll be twenty-three fifty," Holden said after I opened the door.

"Plus a five-dollar delivery fee," Bernard added.

"Come on in, guys," I said.

"It smells damn good," Josh said.

"She put in some paper plates and plastic utensils too," Holden told us.

Bernard jingled the keys to the minivan then dropped them in my hand. "Bet you're glad to have those back."

"Your room was searched thoroughly. Deputies Davidson and Lewis repacked all the personal belongings they found in there, and your luggage is in the van. You'll need to make arrangements with Geneva Louderback to get any personal items left somewhere else in the inn after we've cleared it as a crime scene."

"Like my book," Josh said grumpily.

"My wife also sent you a little surprise, Josh," Holden said. He pulled out a paperback copy of *What Alice Forgot*. "I told her how upset you were that your copy had gone missing, and she wanted you to have it for the long drive home."

Josh smirked in my direction. "I think it was most likely misplaced, but I am so grateful for her thoughtfulness." He'd searched our room high and low looking for the book before we left. I'd told him I put it back where I found it. He wanted to believe me, but it was pretty hard to do when it looked like the book walked off someplace.

"She said it was a great book. It made her think."

"Oh, me too. Please thank your wife for me."

"I will."

"Gabe, do you mind stepping out here for a few minutes? There's something I want to discuss with you before you head back."

"Sure." I looked over at Josh. "I'll be right back."

"I'll keep myself busy with the book while you guys talk shop." Like hell he would. He'd have his ear pressed to the door.

I stepped out onto the concrete walkway in front of the two-story, U-shaped building where all the rooms overlooked the parking lot in the middle of the U. Our room was on the second floor in the center of the hotel. I felt profound relief when I looked over the sketchy-looking metal railing around the perimeter of the second floor and saw our shiny minivan in the parking lot. I only needed five solid hours of sleep then I'd be good to drive home. I'd have Josh read the book out loud to entertain me.

"What's on your mind, fellas?"

"Alice," Holden said.

I raised a brow. "You want to hold a book club before we leave?"

"I think the missing book could be evidence."

"What makes you say that?"

"You said you left the book on the end table next to the wing-back chair, right?" Holden asked.

"I know I put it there."

"Josh said it's not in the room. Books don't disappear on their own," Bernard pointed out. "If he didn't take it, and you didn't take it, then someone else did."

"You're not the only ones missing small items either," Holden added. "Each of the guests reported an inconsequential item was removed from their rooms."

"A hairbrush, cuff links, a bottle of perfume, and a hat to name a few," Bernard told me.

"Not just a hat," Holden said snootily. "It's an expensive fedora purchased in Paris." I didn't need to struggle too hard to figure out whose hat was taken.

"Unless those skeleton keys were universal, the only ones who had access to our rooms were the staff," I told them.

"The keys aren't universal," Holden told me. "There are three keys for each guestroom. They give two keys to guests and one is retained for housekeeping. Geneva Louderback said no one has ever reported stolen items to her before, and she emphatically supports her housekeeping staff."

"Something else odd happened to us the first night we stayed," I said suddenly. I told them about finding the balcony doors open on Saturday morning. "I know for a fact I shut them."

"You think someone came into your room while you slept and opened the balcony doors?"

"I'd convinced myself I hadn't shut the doors all the way, and they had blown open because nothing else made sense. Maybe I didn't want to think about someone creeping around in our room while Josh and I slept." Just saying the words out loud sent a shiver of unease down my spine.

"Are you a sound sleeper?"

"I am, but the sound of an opening door or turning lock would normally wake me up. I doubt very much someone scaled the side of the building and climbed over the balcony rail."

The hotel door opened suddenly behind me. "Secret passages," Josh said suddenly. The three of us turned to face him. "Okay, you caught me eavesdropping, but it wasn't hard to do with these paper-thin doors." Josh rolled his eyes then continued. "Remember how Wanda used secret passages to get the jump on you in the cellar?"

"Wanda?"

"Cellar?"

I could hear the humor and curiosity in their voices, but I thought it was best to stay focused or at least keep Josh focused since he appeared to be on to something. "What makes you think this house has secret passages?"

"There was a lot of uncertainty in our nation during the time the house was built. What if the wealthy owner made sure there was a way for his family to escape from their rooms and hide someplace safe if trouble came knocking at their door? What's something all the rooms had in common?"

Holden and Bernard exchanged a meaningful look.

"Floor-to-ceiling bookshelves," Bernard said.

"Every guest room had them," Holden said in awe. "Why wouldn't Geneva Louderback tell us about them?"

"She hasn't owned the home long. Perhaps it wasn't disclosed to her, or perhaps that level of deceit is so foreign it didn't occur to her," I told them. "Not everyone is a jaded cop."

"Your question now is: who did know? Any of the employees?

What about the guests?" Josh asked. "There was an obvious familiarity between Geneva, Juliette, and a few of the guests."

"Not Bonnie and Clyde," I pointed out. "Juliette was giving them the grand tour after they arrived. Bonnie and Clyde were familiar with George, Georgia, Henry, and Petal, but they didn't act as if they'd stayed at Tarlington House before."

"Damn, who are Bonnie and Clyde again?" Holden asked me.

"Beatrice and Clarence Danner," Bernard answered. "They, along with Michelle and Candace Young, Anna Harris, and Yannis Martin, claimed to be first-time visitors like you."

"I got to know one thing, Detectives," Josh said. "Is Yannis Martin a surgeon?"

"Not even close," Holden replied. "He's a motorcycle mechanic and a very successful one from what I've found."

"I would expect him to have more dexterity like my father-in-law who is a brilliant mechanic," Josh said. "It was obvious he was quite enchanted with Brittany, but I don't see him stabbing her. The man could barely slice through butter, but I guess he could've gotten lucky."

"How'd you know the victim was stabbed?" Bernard asked.

"I coerced the information out of Gabe using my Brenda Leigh skills."

I rolled my eyes. "I shouldn't have said anything to him. I'm sorry, guys."

"I swear I won't say a word about it, Detectives." My look said he was in a lot of trouble.

"So, we have someone possibly sneaking through the passages to steal things and open French doors in the middle of the night," Holden reasoned out loud.

"And stabbing people," Josh added.

Holden snickered. "We didn't forget about that."

"We'll get out of here so you guys can eat and get some sleep," Bernard said. "I'm sure you're eager to leave early."

"Unless you've changed your mind about staying to help," Holden suggested hopefully.

"I haven't," I replied. It was time to get the hell out of there.

Josh and I shook hands with the detectives and thanked them for their thoughtfulness. "Safe travels," they called out as they headed down the steps to the ground level.

Ushering Josh inside, I closed the door, turning the deadbolt and sliding the chain into place though neither would keep out anyone who meant to do us harm. I wished like hell I had my gun. I scooted the chair tucked beneath the small desk so it was wedged beneath the door handle even though it didn't offer much assurance. One good shove and one or more legs were sure to break. I debated moving the dresser in front of the door but decided against it.

By the time I finished, Josh had filled paper plates with delicious-smelling food for both of us. "I'm not sleeping in a separate bed than you," he said around a bite of macaroni salad. "On you, in you, under you, or sleeping on our sides."

I didn't bother cracking jokes or making suggestive comments because I knew his desire to be in the same bed with me had nothing to do with sex. He needed the comfort of my arms holding him tight, or the weight of my body to remind him we were both alive. He needed my body heat to chase away the chill permeating our souls since we found out Brittany was killed. I needed him every bit as much.

After we ate, we wedged ourselves into one twin bed without showering first and fell into a deep sleep. The next time I opened my eyes, sunlight poured in through the cracks around the door and the sliver of space between surprisingly effective blackout curtains. The first thing that occurred to me was I had to piss really bad. I forgot all about my pressing need when I noticed the desk chair was no longer tucked beneath the door handle and realized my husband was no longer in our hotel room.

NINETEEN

Josh

I don't normally consider myself a sneaky or stupid person, but on what was to be the final morning in South Carolina, I proved I could be both of those things when the situation arose. What, pray tell, was the urgent situation that had me sneaking out of the hotel room while Gabe was asleep? My stomach. I was starving by the time Detective Holden delivered our dinner, so I naturally filled up fast. It was like my stomach suddenly shrunk to half its size during the tumultuous hours following Brittany's death.

Would I ever get used to calling her Brittany? I'd heard starvation was used as a method of torture to get suspects to talk, and I could see why it worked.

I checked my GrubHub app, but there were no restaurants delivering so early in the morning. I did a quick search for restaurants and found an adorable donut shop nearby. According to Google Maps, it was only a few blocks away. Wouldn't Gabe love to wake up to warm, delicious donuts and high-octane coffee? We had the keys back, so I could drive the minivan to Dinah's Donuts instead of walking the short distance. A quick trip there and back. I would be perfectly safe. What could go wrong?

I told myself if Gabe so much as stirred while I brushed my teeth and changed clothes, I would go ahead and wake him up so we could grab the donuts on the way out of town. I admit to feeling pissy when Gabe announced we were going home instead of sticking around to help solve the case, but I got over it quickly. First, there was the sexiness of his domineering, protective streak, and the fact he was right. I missed our babies, parents, and friends. I didn't want to spend another second breathing the same air as the phony people we'd met on vacation, and let's not forget, one of those fake fuckers was likely a killer too.

In a way, I guess it was Gabe's fault; he didn't even wiggle a toe, let alone wake up to stop me from pulling a sneaky, stupid stunt. I'd be sure to inform him of it if I got caught too. I quietly let myself out the door then walked down the steps to our van. "Hold up, Josh," said a voice I recognized. I stopped in my tracks and prayed this wouldn't be my last day on earth. I spent absolutely zero time fixing my damn hair before I dashed out, and I couldn't be certain my underwear would be considered good. No one wanted to die in bad underwear. "Just where do you think you're sneaking off to this morning?"

I slowly turned and looked into Henry—William's—vibrant green eyes. "If you must know, I'm going to get breakfast for my husband and me at Dinah's Donuts."

"On foot?"

I pushed the button on the key fob. The minivan's horn beeped and the headlights flashed when it unlocked. "Nope."

"Hey, do you mind if I tag along with you?"

"Actually, William, I do mind. I'm only making a quick stop then coming back here to get my husband so we can get the hell out of Dodge."

"But you're coming back to the hotel, so why does it matter? And why do you guys get to have access to your vehicle while the rest of us don't? How is that fair? Whose dick do I need to suck to get my keys too?"

"Life isn't fair," I replied.

"Why are you so hostile toward me? I thought we made a connection in your room last night."

"You were *grieving* over your wife. We didn't 'make a connection.' What the hell is wrong with you?" Then I realized where the true source of my anger came from. "You have a lot of nerve looking me in the eye and claiming you want to be my friend when just yesterday you slipped a note to my husband. Did you think he wouldn't tell me?"

A sly smile spread across William slash Henry's face. "Aren't you a little curious about what the note said?"

"No," I said, crossing my arms over my chest. "If I had to take a wild guess, I'd say you propositioned my husband."

"You'd be wrong then," he replied flippantly before stepping closer. "Well, partially wrong; I wanted both of you. Still do, if I'm honest."

"Your wife—"

"Of course, I'm upset Brittany is dead, but she was a person who believed in living life to the fullest. She'd want me to celebrate life by fucking until I couldn't fuck any longer."

"You're insane. The whole lot of you are," I said, stepping back toward the safety of my van. "Go away, Henry."

"I prefer indulgent over insane," he said glibly. "It's your loss. Have a nice life, Josh."

I breathed a sigh of relief when he turned and walked away from me. I locked myself in the minivan and took a few seconds to regain my composure before turning the key in the ignition. "Calm down, Josh. Go get the coffee and donuts so we can eat and get the fuck out of here." I glanced up in the rearview mirror as I pulled out of the parking lot. William Henry who-the-fuck-ever was talking to a guy wearing a ball cap low enough to shade his features so I couldn't identify him. There was something familiar about his body language, but I couldn't pull his name out of my tired brain. William Henry didn't look threatened, so I didn't think much of it.

I drove the short distance to Dinah's and stood in line for a solid fifteen minutes before I got up to the counter. My phone rang in my pocket, and I didn't need to check the caller ID to know who was looking for me. I let it go to voicemail while I placed the order then dialed Gabe while the silver fox behind the counter boxed up six of the sexiest donuts I'd ever seen.

"Where the fuck are you?" Gabe snarled into the phone when he picked up.

"Good morning, love of my life."

"Where the fuck are you, Josh?" he asked once more through gritted teeth.

"I'm at the donut shop down the street. Where'd you think I was? The trunk of a car?"

"What's the name of the donut shop?"

"Gabe, I'm not telling you. I'm perfectly safe, and I'll be back in a few minutes with donuts and coffee."

"Tell me—"

I didn't hear the rest of what Gabe had to say because Silver Fox had my order ready. "Gotta go, Gabe. See you in a few." I disconnected the call and smiled at the handsome man patiently waiting for me to grab my goodies and go. "Thank you so much."

Silver Fox winked at me, so maybe my hair wasn't as unfortunate looking as I thought. "Be careful. The coffee is really hot."

My phone rang again immediately, and I answered it as soon as I stepped outside the donut shop so Gabe wouldn't stroke out before I got back to the hotel. "I'm fine, Gabe. I'm almost—"

"William Blake was just shot in the parking lot of our hotel. You are absolutely not safe."

Shock caused me to stop in my tracks just outside the donut shop when I should've hustled to the minivan. "What? I just ran into him. He was casually talking to a guy in the parking lot when I left. Is he—" I couldn't bring myself to finish my question.

"He isn't dead, but he's critical. One of his lungs collapsed, and he was struggling to breathe, so he couldn't tell me who shot him. Whoever shot him probably saw you talking to William before you left. He might think you could identify him. Did William know where you were going?" The fear in Gabe's voice spurred me into action.

"Oh fuck."

"Where are you, Josh?"

"Din—"

"Don't say another fucking word." More menacing than the deep voice behind me was the press of something hard and metal in my lower back. "Hang up the phone. We're going for a ride."

"Josh? Are you still there? Who's with you?" Gabe asked.

Whoever held the gun on me jerked the phone out of my hand, dropped it to the ground, and stomped on it. *Fucker.*

My life didn't flash before my eyes, but I did hear my mother's voice.

"Never get in the car with someone dangerous, Joshy. A moving target is always harder to shoot, but you can increase your chances of survival even more by running in a zig-zag pattern."

I never would've guessed her advice would come in handy.

"If ever you find yourself in trouble, don't holler for help. Yell 'fire' as loud as you can. It's sad, but people aren't always willing to intervene when you're getting attacked. You also throw your assailant off balance, giving you the chance to run."

"Thank you, Roberta Roman," I said out loud.

"Am I supposed to know what that means?"

"FIRE! FIRE! FIRE!" I shouted at the top of my lungs. My assailant jumped back in surprise, giving me enough time to turn and throw my scalding hot coffee in his face.

"Fuck!" he yelled, covering his face with his free hand while waving the gun in the air.

"Gun!" someone yelled. Everyone on the street screamed and ran for safety. Well, all but one.

"I'm going to kill you, you fucking fa—" He didn't get to finish what he was about to say before I drove my knee into his crotch as hard as I could. It was my signature move to take down threats.

Smart people would've run in the zig-zag pattern, but I felt the anger of every homosexual person who had been called ugly names in their lifetime. I got my first real look at my attacker when he fell to the ground holding his junk with his free hand. It was the bellhop from Tarlington House. I poured the second cup of coffee on his face, eliciting more anguished screams from him, but he didn't let go of the gun. I stomped on the wrist of his gun hand as hard as I could, hoping it would cause his hand to go numb. A sickening crunch made me want to puke, but his fingers went slack. I kicked the gun away from his reach and looked around me for help, but everyone had dived into their cars or nearby shops for cover. All except one, sexy-as-fuck man sprinting down the sidewalk toward me. I heard the sirens approaching and knew he'd called for help when he realized something was wrong.

A cop car screeched to a stop, and two officers got out and approached the scene with their weapons drawn. Barking orders for me to move away from the man on the ground. I held my hands in the air and realized I was still holding the bag of donuts and empty drink carrier in my left hand. An unmarked car pulled up right behind them carrying Holden and Bernard. They quickly diverted the focus off me and on to the man on the ground. I'd broken the man's wrist, so he couldn't be cuffed without getting medical treatment first. The responding officers radioed for an ambulance and bagged the gun as evidence. Gabe had stopped a distance from the scene until Holden gave him the okay to approach.

Gabe was a sweaty, panting mess by the time he reached me. "You've got some serious explaining to do," he said, pulling me into his arms and holding me tight. "You scared the fuck out of me. Never again, do you hear me?"

"There won't be a next time because you've promised never to pick a vacation again," I reminded him cheekily. A chuckle rumbled through his chest as his grip tightened even more. "I'm so sorry I scared you, Gabe. I just wanted to surprise you with donuts and coffee."

"Are you cracking cop jokes at a time like this?"

"It wasn't meant to be," I replied honestly.

Silver Fox came out of the donut shop with a new bag of donuts and two fresh coffees. "That was the bravest, and possibly stupidest, thing I've ever seen. The least I can do is replace your empty cups and mangled donuts." We thanked him for his kindness and exchanged the old for the new, and I leaned against Gabe's broad shoulder when Silver Fox went back inside.

Gabe and I munched on the best donuts I'd ever had and sipped our coffee while we watched the ambulance arrive and attend to the injured guy. For a killer, he sure as hell whined and cried a lot.

"Where'd you learn that trick?" Gabe asked.

"What trick? The hot coffee?"

"No, the wrist action." Gabe rolled his eyes when he saw my mind had headed straight for the gutter. "Don't you start with me. I'm still pissed as hell." It was hard to take him serious with powdered sugar on his face and a smear of jelly on the corner of his mouth.

"Cosmetology school."

"You learned how to unarm a person in beauty school?"

"No, Gabe," I said dramatically, "I learned about the nerves traveling through our arms and hands when we were taught the proper manicure techniques at *cosmetology* school. Damage to the radial nerve can cause swelling and numbness in our hands and fingers. I didn't mean to break his wrist though."

"Don't lose a second of sleep over it," Holden said, walking up to us after the ambulance drove off with a police escort.

"He's not remorseful about killing Brittany and attempting to kill her husband," Bernard added.

"He confessed?" Gabe and I both asked.

"Not yet, but it's early still. Speaking of which," Holden said, "why don't you give me your statement of events so you can get on your way home."

The interview didn't take long because my interaction with the man, who turned out to be David the bellhop from Tarlington House, was brief. I talked about my run-in with William and how they appeared to be casually speaking when I pulled out of the parking lot. David hadn't said much before I took him down, so there wasn't much to tell.

Gabe and I were loaded up and back on the highway heading north in less than an hour. It would've been quicker, but Gabe and I had a hard time letting go of each other long enough to function. We'd had a very close call, and it reminded us of how fragile life was and how a person had to live each moment to the fullest because there was no guarantee you'd see the next one. Sometimes, people go out to get ice cream and never come home; sometimes, hateful illnesses rob us of the people we love the most; and sometimes, we fall off the equipment at the gym and lose ten years of memories. I squeezed Gabe's hand on the console between the seats. As tragic as those things are, the walking dead are the saddest, and I don't mean a zombie apocalypse. I'm talking about the people who are alive but don't know it. They've accepted defeat without trying because they haven't realized failure is part of success.

"You haven't said much since we got on the road," Gabe said, breaking into my thoughts.

"I'm just thinking."

"About?"

"How lucky I am, and how much I love our life. I love you so much, Gabe."

"I love you too, Sunshine."

A few years ago, I wasn't capable of this type of conversation, because I was the king of the walking dead. I went through the motions of life and even experienced a lot of success and love from friends and family, but I wasn't living until this man barged into my life.

I released his hand and picked up the paperback copy that Mrs. Holden gave me. "Do you remember what chapter you were on?"

"Twenty," Gabe replied.

"I was only a few chapters ahead of you, but I don't mind reading them again." I opened the book to chapter twenty and began to read out loud, hoping Alice would find the happily ever after she deserved.

TWENTY

Gabe

THERE'S NO PLACE LIKE HOME. THERE'S NO PLACE LIKE HOME. There's no place like home.

Running babies, a barking dog, a meddlesome cat winding her way between my legs, two cussing birds, a feisty ferret, and a huge group of people talking at the same time had never sounded so good or felt so right. All our friends showed up when they heard we'd arrived safely. I wasn't even aware they'd known about the incident because Josh and I agreed not to worry our family and friends.

Adrian knew, of course, because Holden called the station to verify my identity. I knew damn well he didn't tell anyone.

"Wait a minute!" I said, raising the arm not holding Destiny to get their attention. "How'd you guys even know what happened in South Carolina?"

"YouTube," they all said at the same time. Apparently, someone didn't feel brave enough to help Josh, but they didn't mind pointing a camera phone in his direction. That person never wanted to run into me on the street somewhere, because I had words for LuvUrself92, whose channel was filled with ridiculousness.

"We called your cell phone at least a hundred times since the video went viral," Meredith said, gesturing between herself and Chaz. "Why didn't you answer us?" She was so mad she wouldn't let either of us hold Victoria.

"The David guy stomped my phone and broke it," Josh told her. "How viral?"

"Nearly a million views already," Mere replied.

"You could've called Gabe's phone. He used it to let our parents know we were coming home a day early."

Chaz snorted. "Like he'd tell us any of the good details. What the hell happened to you guys this week?"

"It's a long story," I said.

"We like long stories," Kyle replied. "Start at the beginning, and don't give us the crap about being too tired after a long drive. Pizza is on the way, Chaz is going to raid your refrigerator and put a salad together, and Jon brought liquor. You're surrounded by the people who love you, so take a deep breath, release it slowly, and tell us everything you know."

It was a long drive, and I was tired, but I could see they weren't budging without details. Capitulation was my only option unless I had them forcefully removed from our home. "I can't tell you everything I know."

Bernard called me with an update when we were midway

through Kentucky. Josh didn't just break the guy's wrist; he dislocated it at the joint which required surgery. Bernard said they wouldn't be able to interview the guy until he came down off his pain meds. The courts frowned upon the law enforcement community conducting interviews when suspects were high on any substance.

By running his fingerprints through the system, they learned that David used a false identity to get a job at Tarlington House. David was his real first name, but the last name provided to Geneva and the one on his ID was fake. David Thomas was actually David Dubrowski from Atlanta, a convicted felon who was out on parole. David was a con artist, thief, and must've decided to add killer to his resume. Bernard made some calls to the Atlanta PD and talked to the detectives who arrested Dubrowski after a string of robberies and scams to rob the elderly. He learned that the APD suspected his girlfriend, Brittany Alexander, was his accomplice but couldn't prove it.

It seemed ten years in the slammer weren't enough for David to get over Brittany Alexander Blake, aka Petal, but she didn't seem to have trouble moving on from him. William had undergone emergency surgery and appeared to be holding his own in the ICU but wasn't able to talk to Holden and Bernard yet. Olivia, aka Georgia, told detectives Brittany had shown no signs of even recognizing the bellhop, and she believed Brittany would've confided in her if she felt like her life was in danger. He'd only worked for Geneva for less than a month and had gotten along well with the staff at Tarlington House.

The guy must've started stalking Brittany when he was released a few months prior and carefully planned when he would see her again. How did he know about her travel plans? Did he plan to kill her all along, or did he hope they'd pick up where they left off if they ran into each other again? Only David could answer those questions, and I was certain Bernard or Holden would let me know the outcome of their interview. They did find the stolen items in the trunk of his car, and Geneva confirmed that she and all the employees knew of the secret passages inside the home, but all of them interviewed said they never wanted to travel through them for various reasons ranging from lurking spiders and the creepy factor to it feeling like an egregious invasion of privacy. That was how they suspected David was able to spy on guests and steal our things without getting caught.

"Okay, gather around for story time, kids," I said. "Once upon a time…"

"No, Gabe." Josh shook his head emphatically, making Dylan laugh at Daddy. "We don't start off horror stories with those precious words."

"Wait," Bill said suddenly. "Why don't Al and I take the kids outside to swim so they don't hear things they shouldn't."

"Good call," Al said to Bill. "Our wives will be able to repeat this story to us verbatim later."

"Here's the deal," I said after the big kids went outside to swim, earning a nod of approval from my husband. "I wanted to surprise Josh with a murder mystery weekend at this historical inn called Tarlington House. Little did I know, we would become players in a real-life murder mystery." I had everyone's attention then.

I wove them a tale of salacious sex, swingers, and succulent drama. Josh would break in occasionally to add his observations and interactions. We had them eating out of our hands.

"So, they all showed up with fake personas?" my mom asked.

"To a point," I replied. "A few used their real names but made up their jobs while others made everything up. It was like a vacation from their real lives or something." I didn't feel comfortable sharing their real identities while the investigation was still ongoing. It was something that could hurt careers and negatively impact lives. I thought about Candace and how she played a young Hollywood starlet with the baby-soft voice when she was really an astrophysicist who worked for NASA. Her mother, Michelle, or Mitzi for short, truly was a former beauty queen like she'd said. She had been Miss Alabama and first runner-up for Miss America.

The feud between Brittany, aka Petal, and Beatrice, aka Bonnie, started in college. After David went to prison, it appeared Brittany had tried to clean her life up. She enrolled at Georgia University where she met Beatrice and her brother, Clarence, and of course, William who was Beatrice's fiancé at the time. William and Clarence both fell in love with Brittany, but she chose William, leaving the Danner siblings bitter and angry. Was it a coincidence the four of them chose to attend the Tarlington House murder mystery event, or was something else going on? The Danners insisted it was a shocking coincidence, and the detectives didn't have evidence to prove otherwise. Dylan and Olivia, aka George and Georgia, were exactly as they claimed to be. Dylan was an investment banker rolling in big money and Olivia was his bored wife. They liked engaging in the swinging lifestyle and had no intention of changing their ways. As Dylan pointed out, their swapping couples or engaging in orgies had nothing to do with Brittany's death.

By the time we were done telling the story, our friends had demolished the pizza. Josh and I were too tired and overwhelmed to eat, but I did enjoy a few beers, and Josh drank two glasses of wine.

"It's a lot to take in," Harley said, shaking his head.

"Tell me about it," Josh said dryly. "It felt like we were trapped in an episode of *The Twilight Zone*."

"It sounds like the first few days were fun though," Bertie said.

Josh smiled happily at me. "They were the best, but we're so glad to be home now."

"That's our cue to get out," Meredith said.

"We didn't get to hold Tori," Josh said with a pout.

"I'll bring her back tomorrow after you've had a good night of rest. You can smooch her little face while I float in the pool."

"Fine, but just one little kiss tonight," Josh pleaded. "I

apologized profusely for worrying you."

"Okay," Meredith agreed. Josh leaned over and kissed Tori's head. Then he inhaled deeply. "Hey now. I didn't say anything about you snorting her baby essence up your nose."

Meredith carried Tori over to me so I could kiss her goodnight too. This hectic week didn't do anything to change my mind about growing our family. In fact, it made me eager to make it happen quicker. I just needed to find the right time to start convincing my husband.

"I'm ready for another baby," I said after I got back inside from seeing our friends and family off. Our folks had offered to stay the night so we could sleep in, but the truth was, I wasn't turning loose of our kids. Josh didn't know it yet, but I was breaking the sage rule of no kids in bed.

Josh tipped his head to the side. I knew he was thinking of everything we experienced the past week and the lessons we learned—both in fiction and real life. Waiting for the perfect moment was a setup for disappointment because no such thing existed. There was only now. "Okay, but I want some things in return."

"I'm listening," I said.

"I don't want you to throw a fit when I have a celebration next week thanking Trent and Tucker for taking such good care of Meredith when she went into labor at the salon. I'm telling you I saw some awesome sparks between them, and I'm going to—"

"Meddle?"

"*Encourage*," Josh replied.

"Fine," I said. "One dinner. Now, what are the rest of your demands?"

"I want to start a monthly book club at our house."

"Deal." I couldn't imagine why he thought I'd protest that one. What the hell did he plan on reading, and would there be scene reenactments?

"There goes the neighborhood," Sassy squawked.

Savage started singing "Highway to Hell" and bopping his head to the imaginary beat.

Josh and I exchanged knowing looks. Our dads were teaching them new material while we were gone, and the birds were biding their time before they revealed it. I'd already been called a fucknugget, Josh was called a twat waffle, and they told us both to shove a cock in it. The birds were obviously pissed about our absence.

"Damn, I love this life," Josh and I both said.

EPILOGUE

Josh

Three months later...

"How much longer until you turn off your curling iron for the night?" Gabe asked when I answered his call. Not hello, not how are you, and not I miss you. He wanted to know how long before I got home. I'd just finished with my last client, but I wasn't so eager to share that detail with him yet.

"Hello to you too, Gabe." My tone expressed what my polite

words could not. Mrs. Sanderson's eyes met mine in the mirror. We rolled them together in commiseration.

"He probably wants to know what's for dinner," she whispered.

"I do not," Gabe groused. "I got a call from our caseworker at DCS. They have—"

"Oh my God! We're getting a baby tonight?" Everyone in the salon started clapping.

"Well, um…"

"Two babies?" I asked.

"Um…"

"Gabriel!"

Mrs. Sanderson chuckled as she rose to her feet and removed her cape. She kissed my cheek and wished me luck before heading to the counter to pay and book her next service.

"Just tell me what time I can swing by and pick you up. Our parents are here with Dylan and Destiny now."

"I just need to sweep up my mess, and I—"

"Be right there," Gabe said excitedly and hung up. I'd chosen to walk to work that morning to enjoy the autumn weather before it turned nasty.

"What's going on?" Mere asked.

"I think Gabe and I are about to adopt a basketball team." Why did I sound so calm? The deal was we would adopt one more child and maybe another one in the distant future. I didn't even know how many kids Gabe was talking about, but I realized it didn't matter. I was calm because it felt right.

"See you all in the morning," I said after I finished sweeping up my station.

"You better call me later tonight," Mere said.

"That's a given. Love you, Mere."

I headed out front to wait for Gabe. I loved the crisp October air and couldn't wait for Trick or Treat to show off the cutest toddler Halloween costumes ever. I found ideas on Pinterest on how to decorate the little red wagons Destiny and Dylan would ride in. Then I realized my carefully orchestrated plans would need to be modified based on the outcome of our evening.

Gabe barely stopped our snazzy new minivan in front of the salon long enough for me to get in. "I think you left tire marks back there, Captain Caravan."

Gabe ignored my crack and went right to the heart of the matter. "I know this isn't what we originally planned, but these kids have been through so much. We can't separate them."

"What if they don't like us? This isn't a unilateral decision we can make, Gabe." I could see he had his hopes up high, and I couldn't bear to see him hurt. "Let's meet the kids and see how it goes. No pressure."

"Yeah, you're right."

Marsha was waiting for us when we arrived at the Carter County Department of Children Services. "Hello, guys," she said softly. "I know you were thinking about adopting a baby, but you're the first family I thought of when the Newman siblings arrived today." She sounded so nervous like we might reject the kids outright, and I hated it so much.

I placed my hand on her forearm. "Breathe, Marsha."

"I told Gabe about the circumstances requiring our intervention. Did he have time to discuss it with you?"

I shook my head. "I don't need to know the details right now. I want to meet the kids without anything clouding my judgment." The kids deserved someone seeing *them* and not their tragedy. "Let's go say hello."

"Fair enough, but I need to point out that I don't believe this will be a temporary situation. These kids will need a permanent home where they will find patience and unconditional love." Marsha led us to a room in the rear of the building. My previous calmness fled, and my heart raced as I neared the door. I knew something amazing awaited me—us—and the feeling of rightness intensified. Then Marsha opened the door, and my heart caught in my throat.

"Josh and Gabe," Marsha said calmly, "I'd like you to meet Darius, Matteo, and Rochelle Newman. Darius is seven, Matteo is five, and Rochelle is three."

Rochelle was curled into a tight ball on Darius's lap, and Matteo leaned into his side. Rochelle smiled around the thumb in her mouth, Matteo looked hopeful, and Darius had the world-weariness I associated with someone much older than a small kid. I wanted to rush in there and hug them all, but I didn't want to frighten them.

"Hey, guys," I said, hoping my cheerfulness sounded natural. Rochelle waved her free hand at me. I sat down on the floor because I didn't want to seem intimidating by standing over them. Gabe followed my lead which Rochelle found funny. Go ahead and giggle, sweet angel, you'll have him wrapped around your finger in no time.

"I like your shirt," I told Darius. He looked down at his *Black Panther* T-shirt and shrugged. He wouldn't be easy to win over, but it would be a true thing of beauty when we earned his trust.

"I adore your braids, Rochelle." She giggled some more and gripped one of her braids.

"Do you like baseball?" Gabe asked Matteo who wore a Reds jersey. He looked to his older brother for approval before responding. After Darius nodded, Matteo faced Gabe and cracked a huge grin that we assumed meant yes.

We spent an hour in the tiny room talking to the three children I knew would someday share our last name. We told them about our jobs, our kids, and the pets we had at home. We asked about school and what their hobbies were. Rochelle had wiggled out of Darius's arms at one point and plopped herself in Gabe's lap. I could tell he wanted to hold her tight but worried he would frighten her. Tears burned the back of my eyes when Gabe looked up and caught me watching them together. The boys weren't as trusting, but they were older and probably witnessed more than their sister had. Eventually, Matteo got curious and sat on the floor beside me. He leaned into me like he'd done his brother, and I gently placed my hand on his thin shoulder.

Darius wanted to believe, but he was just too afraid. "You must be an amazing big brother," I said. He just shrugged. "How would you like to be a big brother to two more kids?" Darius's eyes widened a little, but he still didn't speak. I did notice his shrug was a little less emphatic. He was the only one who hadn't talked to us yet, but it didn't worry me. "Are you willing to try?" I held my breath waiting for him to answer. It was subtle when it came, but there was no mistaking his nod.

We weren't prepared to take home three kids who required booster seats, so we borrowed them from the county. I'd have a lot of shopping to do to prepare rooms for the kids. I was concerned about not having their bedrooms set up already, but Marsha took me aside and told me the three of them wouldn't want to be separated on the first night in a strange place anyway. We had two guest bedrooms already set up, so they could use one of them and help me pick out stuff for their rooms the next day. And I couldn't forget Halloween costumes. I suddenly didn't want to plan a cohesive theme with costumes that coordinated. I wanted the kids to pick out what they wanted to wear. Sometimes a person needed to embrace the messy and chaotic. We needed to be the bright colors in an often drab and dreary world.

It was pitch-black out by the time we left DCS, and the air temperature seemed to have dropped at least ten degrees. We secured everyone in their booster seats then shut the sliding doors. The looks Gabe and I exchanged when we sat in our seats said so much. Things like I love you, thank you for believing in me, and we're in this together. Forever. Gabe was a man who saw my true colors and loved every single one of them. I reached over and cupped his jaw affectionately, brushing my thumb over his lips.

"Kids, there's one rule I need to tell you right now before we get home," I told them.

"Oh, brother," Darius said drily, speaking for the first time. "What's the rule?" Gabe smiled at me because even those few words were a huge victory.

"You are never allowed to repeat what the birds say."

"Huh?" all three of them asked.

"You'll see what he means," Gabe told them. Then to me he mouthed the words, "I love you."

I thought it was quite possible my heart would explode from all the love swelling inside it. This beautiful man sitting beside me wore many titles; he was my husband, best friend, lover, papa to our children, my ride or die, and my happily ever after. I opened my mouth to speak, but no words came out.

"I know, Sunshine." And he did because I made certain he knew how much I adored him, and I vowed there would never be a day where he doubted my devotion to him and our family.

Gabe started the van and drove us toward a future that was certain to be chaotic, messy, and filled with more love than I ever dreamed possible.

The End!

Want to be the first to know about my book releases and have access to extra content? You can sign up for my newsletter here: eepurl.com/dlhPYj

My favorite place to hang out and chat with my readers is my Facebook group. Would you like to be a member of Aimee's Dye Hards? We'd love to have you! Click here: www.facebook.com/groups/AimeesDyeHards

OTHER BOOKS BY AIMEE NICOLE WALKER

Only You

The Fated Hearts Series
Chasing Mr. Wright, Book 1
Rhythm of Us, Book 2
Surrender Your Heart, Book 3
Perfect Fit, Book 4
Return to Me, Book 5
Always You, Book 6
Any Means Necessary, Book 7

Curl Up and Dye Mysteries
Dyeing to be Loved
Something to Dye For
Dyed and Gone to Heaven
I Do, or Dye Trying
A Dye Hard Holiday

Road to Blissville Series
Unscripted Love
Someone to Call My Own
Nobody's Prince Charming
This Time Around
Smoke in the Mirror

The Lady is Mine Series
The Lady is a Thief

Coauthored with Nicholas Bella
Undisputed
Circle of Darkness (Genesis Circle, Book 1)
Circle of Trust (Genesis Circle, Book 2)

Standalone Novels
Second Wind

ACKNOWLEDGMENTS

First, I need to thank my husband and children for their constant support and encouragement. It's not easy living with a writer who often disappears into a fictional world for long periods of time. They do so many things to help me out so that I can realize my dream. I love you guys more than words can ever express.

To my creative dream team, thanks seem hardly enough for all that you do. Miranda Vescio of V8 Editing and Proofreading, thank you for your tireless work, feedback, and many laughs while editing. Jay Aheer of Simply Defined art is an incredible artist, and I love how she brings my words to life. Stacey Blake of Champagne Formats is also an amazing artist who does incredible interior formatting, illustrating, and designing for e-books and paperbacks. Let's not forget Judy Zweifel of Judy's' Proofreading. She does an amazing job of finding the tiniest details that make a book shine.

To my lovely PA, Michelle Slagan. I'm not sure how I ever did this without you. I love you to the moon and back!

When I started writing this book, I asked my Dye Hards group to give me suggestions for the other players who would appear during the murder-mystery weekend. I want to thank everyone for their input, but I must give special mention to Joscelyn Smith (Henry & Petal), Rachel Zertuche (Mitzi & Candace), Minskat Petersen (Yanny & Laurel), and Racheal Yunk (Bonnie & Clyde) for their submissions. I hope you enjoyed reading the storylines I created for your characters.

Lastly, I am so grateful for my beta readers and the honest feedback they provide me. Thank you for all that you do, Racheal, Kim, Laurel, Michael, Brittany, Dana, Michelle, and Jodie.

ABOUT THE AUTHOR

Ever since she was a little girl, Aimee Nicole Walker entertained herself with stories that popped into her head. Now she gets paid to tell those stories to other people. She wears many titles—wife, mom, and animal lover are just a few of them. Her absolute favorite title is champion of the happily ever after. Love inspires everything she does, music keeps her sane, and coffee is the magic elixir that fuels her day.

I'd love to hear from you.

You can reach me at:

Twitter—twitter.com/AimeeNWalker

Facebook—www.facebook.com/aimeenicole.walker

Blog—AimeeNicoleWalker.blogspot.com

www.ingramcontent.com/pod-product-compliance
Lightning Source LLC
Chambersburg PA
CBHW031426250626
47155CB00004B/1646